Phas‹   
Short Fictions

Volume 1

Phase 5, Phase 5 Publishing, LLC
PO Box 3131
Asheville, NC 28802,
www.phase5publishing.com

First Edition May 2015
Previously published in *The Phase 5 Monthly Review*, various
issues.
Edited by Phase 5 Publishing, LLC
Anthology. Science Fiction; Fantasy. Vampires, interdimensional
travelers, other worlds, aliens, post-apocalyptic, supernatural,
ghosts, alien worlds, telepathy, telekinesis, altered states of
being, urban fantasy
Teen and Adult readers: Non-graphic violence and death,
vampirism, suggested sexual situations, infrequent profanity,
artificial intelligence, theft and intent to do harm.
Phase 5 Elements: Science Fiction 1, Fantasy 2, Lessons 78
ISBN 978-1-942342-90-8 $9.99
Printed and Distributed by Lightning Source, a member of
the Ingram Content Group, in the United States of America and
worldwide
Also available as an ebook
Coded and Distributed by Lulu through the Ingram Content
Group, in the United States of America and worldwide

Acknowledgements

The Editor thanks the authors for their patience and continued journey with Phase 5. The path may have altered and taken some unplanned detours, but the destination remains the same. Thank you for accompanying me.

Foreword

Welcome to Phase 5's first annual anthology of short fiction. Packed within these pages are civic minded vampires, life coaches who might be ghosts (maybe), people with dangerous talents and intent, a young woman who loses herself totally to love, post-apocalyptic descendants (and I use that term loosely) surviving and thriving in what's left of the world, a young lady preyed upon by a dimensional traveler, and an aged professor on an alien world seeking to maintain the peace of his home. These stories span science fiction, fantasy, and speculative fiction of many themes and subgenres. However, we find the characters within them are seeking similar goals within their disparate worlds. Join them on their journeys, if only for a step or two of each, and enjoy this first visit to the short fictions of the wide-flung worlds, times, and places of Phase 5.

Table of Contents

Doriann's Choice

By Allen L. Wold

Shadae strode out onto the starlit balcony. The wind which ruffled his hair and beard brought the smell of the city, the scent of the surrounding forest and, this always surprised him, the faint smell of snow from the nearby mountains. He leaned on the stone railing, and gazed down at the lamp-lit street below him.

Movement to his right caught his attention. A small woman stood in the corner, cloaked and hooded. Light from the glass doors behind them fell on her near side.

"I'm sorry," he said. "I didn't mean to intrude."

She started at his first words, and turned toward him a face so remarkably ugly that it took his breath away, almost before he could finish. He suppressed any other reaction.

"I sometimes have to get away from people," he went on, with a half a nod toward the crowd talking, drinking and laughing inside.

"Me, too," she said. Her voice was an interesting contralto, made more complex by unexpressed emotions. She turned her face away into the darkness.

He knew what she was going to do, even before she climbed up onto the railing.

There was no time to think about it. He jumped over the railing toward her, even as she fell. He caught her around the waist and chest before they had fallen half way, careful, even in this circumstance, where he put his hands. She was surprised and stiffened, but did not struggle as he twisted them upright. She was not heavy, even so it took all his strength to slow them before his feet hit the cobblestones. He flexed his knees to absorb the shock, then straightened and set her down.

She stood, gasping, her hood fallen back, staring at nothing. He took a step away from her. It was hard to determine her age, he guessed her to be not yet twenty.

"How... how did you do that?" she asked at last, looking up at him.

"It's a talent," he said. "I don't know how it works. I don't like to show it off. It's nearly gotten me killed a couple times."

She was staring at him, at his eyes, his mouth, his chest, then his eyes again. Then she abruptly turned away. "I'm sorry," she said.

"There is no need to be."

She would not turn toward him. "You shouldn't have," she said. "It wasn't easy to...."

"I'm sure it wasn't," he said. "Please understand. I don't think you should, but if you must, do it where you won't horrify the people who find you."

The street had been empty when they had descended, but there were three casual evening strollers coming toward them now. She glanced at them, then pulled her hood over her head and turned to the wall.

He leaned back against it, watched the man and two women approach, and smiled at them as they passed.

"You don't approve," she said intensely when they had gone. She threw her hood back and faced him. "Look at me," she said. "People have tried to kill me, too."

He would not let himself look away. Perhaps he should not have spoken, but at least she was talking to him. "My name is Shadae," he said. He held out his hand.

His proffered hand surprised her, but she took it. Her grip was firm. "Doriann," she said. "I'm- I guess I should thank you, after all."

"I cannot imagine what it must be like," he said, "but death severely limits your choices."

Another man approached from the opposite direction. There was not a lot of light in this part of the street, but the ugliness of her face was all too visible. As soon as she became aware of the passerby, she started to conceal herself again, then stopped, and made herself stand so that he could see her as he went by.

The man's reaction was only what might be expected. He glanced, then took a surprised look, then kept his eyes averted as he walked past, his face stiff. He looked over his shoulder at her once, shuddered, and hurried away. She stood motionless, enduring it.

Shadae watched her. Her unhappiness did not improve her appearance. He wanted very much to turn away when she looked up at him, but he did not. "How did you manage to get up to the balcony?" he asked her.

"Back stairs. They wouldn't let me in the front." That was on the other side of the building, where there was a lot more light.

"Did you come up just to jump?"

"Yeah." She looked at the ground, clearly unaccustomed to prolonged attention.

"How old are you?"

"Eighteen." She paused, showing her pain, and met his gaze as if testing his resolve. "My mother exposed me when I was born. But I'm strong. After listening to me cry for three nights, she finally brought me in. But she wouldn't nurse me herself. She made a false teet and fed me goat's milk. My father wouldn't look at me at all, of course." She sighed. "There's no point in talking about it."

"What made you decide?"

"Oh, there was a boy. I never spoke to him or anything. Mostly he didn't pay any attention. People were used to me. They paid no attention, like I wasn't there." She unconsciously glanced in the direction the man had gone. "But the more I thought about him...."

He looked away from her now. A man with a talent like his was seen as a resource to be exploited, by criminals and the power hungry, or someone to be feared by almost anybody. But all he had to do was not use that talent, and none would know. For Doriann, there was no escape. "How long have you been running?" he asked her.

"Three years or so."

"How do you manage?" He was afraid he would not like the answer.

"I steal. I almost never get caught. And, when I am, I show them my face, and that gives me time to run away."

"Sleep in the open?"

"Wherever I can." There was no resentment in her voice, just resignation.

"Your clothes don't look it."

"I have a couple changes. I didn't bother to bring them with me." She looked up at the balcony sixty feet overhead. "Won't they miss you up there?"

"Some of them, probably, for a little while, but they won't care."

He could read the question in her face.

12

"I wasn't invited, but nobody knows that. I got what I came for. It was time for me to leave anyway."

"Are you a thief?"

Their gazes met again, and his expression remained steady. "No. Where are you staying?"

She looked away.

"How do you eat?"

"I can usually find a restaurant where the trash isn't too bad."

"What would happen if you went back home?"

"I'm not going back."

"I'm not suggesting it. I just thought it might be easier to live where people are used to you."

She looked away, then looked back. "You don't turn away," she said.

He looked down at her feet, the worn boots, the stained trousers. The cloak concealed the rest of her. She must have slept under it often. When he looked back at her face, the shock was not as bad as the first time. "It sometimes isn't easy to be a gentleman," he said, "but it's important to me. There is no reason for me to add to your discomfort, or for you even to know that I might."

It was her turn to look away.

"Traditionally," he said, "if you save someone's life, you are responsible for them thereafter." She turned back to him, with a look of dismay. He smiled, and said, "I'm not going to impose on you. But when have you last eaten?"

"Hah? Just a couple hours ago."

"If I walk away, will you try it again?"

"No. I'm not in the mood."

"I hope that's an improvement." He smiled again, and started to leave.

"Can you really fly?" she asked.

"No, not fly." He looked along the street in both directions. There was no one to witness. If there was someone looking from a darkened window, he could not tell. He thought about himself, in that peculiar way he did. It was like thinking about raising his arm, except it was his whole body. It took an effort, of course, but he went up. Not weightless, just up. Not suspended or supported or dangling, just up. Three inches, six inches, twelve, eighteen, two feet. There was no need to go higher.

She stared at him. There was something in her eyes. "Is it hard?"

"It takes effort, like carrying a weight takes effort, that's all." He settled back to the ground. "I don't usually let people see. I learned to be cautious a long time ago."

"I can do something," she said. The way she said it was significant, as if she were afraid of it, not bragging.

"What can you do?" he asked her.

She hesitated. "Have you got a penny?"

He knew what she was going to do. He took a few coins out of his pocket and, without looking at them, held them out on the open palm of his hand. She looked at them, and a penny came up out of his hand, as if held by invisible fingers, nimble fingers like those of a juggler. Then it went back down so gently that he almost could not feel it.

He put the coins back in his pocket. His smile felt different this time. "We need to talk. Where are you staying?"

This time she trusted him with an answer. "In a culvert. It's dry."

"Would you be comfortable there?"

"It's dry, not comfortable."

"That's not what I meant."

"Oh. Oh. Ah, wherever."

"The inn where I'm staying is not far from here."

"Okay. I'm not afraid of you." It was half declaration and half something else, something he could not read in her eyes. He presumed it to be the resignation he had heard in her voice earlier.

"That's good. You have no reason to be, but you don't know that." He started walking, she fell in step beside him.

"But I do. No man would ever touch me. Not even with a bag over my head. So I've been told."

"That's cruel," he said.

"It's one thing I don't have to worry about. A couple guys found me one time, under a bridge. They grabbed me when it was dark, then one of them struck a light. They went away very quickly. For that one moment, I was glad I look the way I do."

They came to an intersection. The street they were on angled one way, the other street teed at the angle and went off in the other direction. They went that way.

"Why were you up there?" Doriann asked.

That was his business, but he had decided to teach her how to use her talent, so it would be unfair to keep the secret. "I wanted to find out where a particular man lived," he said.

"Did you?"

"I did."

They walked a short way in silence she asked, "What will you do?"

He did not want to answer, but the trouble with engaging yourself with people was that they began to deserve more than your simple respect and courtesy. "Some years ago, this man, Imanni, falsified some documents and had my parents evicted from their farm, which had been in our family for generations. I was away at the time, which is probably just as well, since I couldn't have prevented it, and he might have killed me for opposing it. When I found out about it, my mother had died, and my father was living off the charity of neighbors." His expression had not substantially changed, and his voice was controlled enough to not betray him.

"If — if this man took your farm, wouldn't he be there?"

"He set a vassal in place, a man and his wife and three children, and two other men who help work the farm, but who are also armed fighters. When I came back, and found strangers in my house, I… got upset. I got away, but Imanni knows I'm alive and looking for him."

"You sound so calm."

"It's been ten years. And anger clouds your judgment, sometimes more than fear does. This way."

He led her around some more corners. In the middle of the block was an inn. It was a small establishment, but it had a passage along the side to a stableyard. Doriann drew her cowl down further over her face as they went inside.

There was a small public room on one side of the narrow lobby, and a registration desk along the other. The man behind the desk looked up when they came in. Doriann's face was covered, but he knew she was a woman. He smirked, and made a rude gesture, which Doriann must have seen because she flinched slightly. Shadae strode to the desk, leaned across it, seized the clerk's upper arm and said, very quietly, "If you were a friend of mine, I'd knock you down for that. You're not a friend of mine. If you do that again, I'll knock you down twice." He let go of the clerk's arm, rejoined Doriann, and led her to the back of the foyer and up the stairs.

"I'm sorry," he said as he opened the door to his room.

"Would you really have done that?"

He looked down at her and smiled. "He'll never know," he said. "But if I thought it would actually teach him some manners, yes, I would have." He gestured to the chair.

"Are you," she asked as she sat, "a very violent man?" No fear in her voice, no expression he could read on her face.

He took off his jacket, tossed it on the pillows, and sat at the foot of the bed. "I have been, from time to time. It's not something I enjoy, but I don't shrink from it either."

"You weren't always like that."

"No."

She met his gaze, as he met hers. He did not allow himself to think about how ugly she was, more visibly so in good light.

"You said we had to talk," she said.

He looked away from her as he put his hand into his pocket. He took out a large coin, and held it out in the palm of his hand.

She understood what he wanted her to do. She looked at the coin, and after a brief moment it rose up into the air, as if under its own power. It floated there, a few inches above his palm, then it flipped over slowly, heads for tails, three times, then settled back down on his palm. He closed his hand over it, but did not put it back in his pocket.

"What are you thinking of when you do that?" he asked her.

"I," she moistened her lips. People had been lynched for doing less than that small display. "I think about reaching out, picking it up, turning it over."

"With your hand?"

"Yes... yes."

"Raise your arm." He showed her what he wanted her to do. "Do you think about the muscles in your arm, your shoulder, when you do that, how they contract and pull on the joints?"

She looked confused. "No, I just raise my arm."

"If you hold your arm out, and think about all those muscles and joints, it becomes very difficult to do anything meaningful or useful. If you don't think about it, but just do it, it just happens, and you can do almost anything."

"Is it like that when you float?"

"It's like lifting a heavy weight. I have to concentrate my energy, but I don't think about what's moving, what I'm doing, other than lifting myself up." He held out the coin again.

She understood, intellectually, what he had told her. She looked at the coin in his hand. After a moment, she looked up at his face. She must have been reassured by what she saw. Her face relaxed and, to his surprise, became strangely appealing. Her anguish and despair made her ugliness worse.

The coin came up off his hand, then smacked hard against the wall behind the head of the bed. He did not turn. The coin did not fall to the floor. She was staring at him, surprised, breathing hard through her open mouth. He smiled, and the coin came gracefully around the other side of his head, and settled onto this still open hand.

"Oh my," she said.

"Very few of us have the talent," he said gently. "Many who discover they have it die at the hands of people who are afraid of them. It's not something you display casually."

"I know. I've never let anyone see."

"You understand the risk. You need to practice. You must never be careless."

"No, I know how to be careful."

"Of course. The talent is not a simple thing. I am especially good at lifting myself up into the air. I can also pass unnoticed sometimes. Sometimes I can see a few seconds into the future. I cannot move objects as well as you can, beginner that you are."

"I," She stopped herself, stood up, paced to one side of the room, then to the other, then back to the chair and sat down. "I want to learn," she said.

"You will."

"Will you help me? I mean, I know you have things to do." She clasped her hands in lap, anxiety masking her hope.

"I do. And I will do them. If you want to come with me, I will do what I can."

Her next question was more hesitant. "What do I …?"

"I want nothing from you. Just finding another person with talent is reward enough. Do you understand?"

"I think so. I won't get in your way."

"I know that."

"Is that part of the talent?"

"It is. I'm not as good at it as someone I know.

What are you going to do now?"

She stared blankly at him.

"Are you going back to your culvert? Or will you stay here?"

"I have things there." Even as she said the words, her eyes danced enviously around the room.

"I'll come with you."

They left his room. Doriann pulled her cowl over her face. As they went through the lobby, Shadae glanced at the clerk, who was carefully busy with something behind the counter.

Doriann led the way. She did not speak. Shadae did not try to break her silence.

They came to a place where a drainage ditch ran along the side of the road. The road itself rose to a crossing with another street, but the ditch became an enclosed culvert passing under it. The bottom was sloped, the edge near the road a few inches higher than the rest and, at the present at least, quite dry. Doriann did not enter immediately, but stood, clearly visible to whoever might be inside, just outside the opening. If someone were in there, she could get away quickly up the bank beside her. There was no one.

She went in. Shadae followed, a few feet behind her, keeping his own senses sharp. About half way along, she stooped at a darker place on the ground, felt around with her hands, then stood, holding a loose bundle. She came back, and Shadae led her out of the culvert. When they got to where there was some light, she knelt, arranged her few belongings, and tied them into a much neater bundle, which she slung by a cord over her shoulder.

"Okay," she said.

When they got back to the inn, Shadae went to

the clerk, who was not happy to see him. "Send a cot up to my room," Shadae told him.

"Ah, that will cost-"

"I know. Do it."

They went up to his room. Ten minutes later, two women came with a folding cot and blankets. The cot had a mattress, and looked comfortable enough. After the maids finished setting it up, Shadae stood to go sit on it, but Doriann got to it first.

"No," she said. "This is better than anything I've slept on for three years. You keep your bed."

Shadae smiled, made a slight bow, and said, "As you wish."

Doriann did not want to eat breakfast in the common room, so Shadae had their meal brought to his room. He was a bit wary of showing too much kindness. He did not want whatever gratitude Doriann might feel to cloud her judgment. But as far as he could tell, she accepted his generosity in the spirit in which it was intended.

"Where is this man you're looking for?" she asked while they ate.

"In the city. I have his address."

"Will you see him today?"

"I will. This afternoon."

She said nothing.

"I'm going to look around the neighborhood first," he said. "I've never been there. I want to see what it's like-"

"Of course. In case you have to leave quickly."

"Exactly."

She was silent. She did not want to be left

behind.

"You want to come along?" he asked her.

"Yes, please." She was going to say something about keeping out of his way, but decided not to.

"I'll be staying here tonight," he said, "assuming all goes well. After that, I don't yet know."

"It doesn't matter to me," she said.

While Shadae waited in the hallway, Doriann changed into cleaner clothes. Then they left the inn, and went to a residential part of town, where houses were set back from the streets behind little gardens, and were separated from each other by passages to back yards.

"What will you do?" Doriann asked.

"Talk to him first."

"Do you think he'll give you your farm back?"

"No."

She was silent a moment. Then she asked, "Will you kill him?"

"That would not serve my purpose." He glanced at her. "There *is* more to my life than this farm," he said, "however important it may be to me. I've not spent the whole of my time looking for this man."

"What do you do?"

"Different things. Stocked a warehouse. Assembled furniture. Tended bar. Worked in a library."

"Really? Doing what?"

"Acquiring books, cataloging, keeping the shelves."

"Did you like it?"

"I did, as a matter of fact. I was a deputy sheriff for a while. Shipping clerk. Construction foreman. The library was the best."

"If you get the farm back, what will you do?"

"I don't know."

Shadae stopped in front of a rather nice house. It was not at all exceptional for the neighborhood. The front garden was maybe fifteen feet deep with flowering shrubs on either side, a gate to the passage as well as one to the garden and beds of flowers, some in bloom, on either side of a curving walkway of riverstones. The house had three floors and a cellar, a bay window on the ground floor, curtained, the entrance in a recess on the right.

"This may not be the right man," Shadae said.

"Will you know if it is?"

He did not answer. She did not have to ask again.

He opened the gate. After a moment of hesitation she followed him up the path to the steps to the front door. She was afraid, but she was going to come in with him. He had not expected that, but he did not say anything to stop her. He stood in front of the door for a moment, then he knocked. He was about to knock again when he heard footsteps approaching. The man who answered the door was a servant.

"I'd like to speak with Imanni," Shadae said. "Tell him it's about the Bardain farm."

The servant's eyes flickered. The name meant something to him. "Come in, please," he said, and stepped back from the door, into a broad entrance hall, with stairs along one side going to the upper floors. He glanced only once at Doriann, who kept her cowled face discreetly averted.

They were shown into the front room, a parlor for receiving guests. There was no other door. It was a comfortable room, the furniture was good but not expensive. Doriann chose a chair in the front corner, where she could sit with her back half turned to the door. Shadae looked around the room briefly, then stood in the middle, waiting.

They did not wait long. The man who came in was fair complexioned, with short hair and close trimmed beard, in his middle fifties. He was cautious, but not apprehensive. After all, some people might have a legitimate reason for enquiring after the farm. "How can I help you?" he asked. He was a tenor.

"I'm Shadae of Bardain farm," Shadae said.

Imanni's face did not change at first, as if he had not heard, or had not understood. Then he said, with annoyance, "What do you intend to do about it?"

"Get it back. If you can write up false deeds proving it belongs to you, then you can write up another giving it back to me."

"And why would I do that?"

"Come outside and I'll show you."

"I'll do no such thing." He turned away.

Shadae took three steps, grabbed Imanni around the waist, lifted him over his head, carried him up to the ceiling, ten feet above the floor, and let him fall. He descended quickly, grabbed Imanni again by the belt, at the small of his back, carried him up to the ceiling again, and let him drop, so that he hit the floor on his shoulder and hip. He picked him up a third time, and held him face up against the ceiling, but with his head a bit lower than his hips, and said, "I guess I can show you what I want to right here," and let him fall, so that he landed on his shoulders, which stressed but did not break his neck. Then Shadae descended again to stand where he had been, in the middle of the room. The door opened, the butler looked in, something moving very fast hit him just above his left eye, and he crumpled to the floor, unconscious. The door behind him, seemingly by itself, closed.

Shadae, not as surprised as someone else might have been, looked over his shoulder at Doriann. Her face, so ugly it startled him, despite the time he had spent with her, was flushed. She was staring at the butler, but she felt his glance and looked back at him. Neither of them felt the need to say anything.

Imanni, lying on his back, was gasping, one hand at his neck, the other clawing at the air above his waist. Shadae went to stand at his head, and when Imanni finally took notice of him, he said, "My mother died. My father is suffering on charity. There's nothing you can do about that. But you can evict the family who lives there now, and give the farm back to me. I hope you'll do something nice for them, to compensate them for their trouble, but that's your business. Now, how do we go about giving me my farm back?"

"I can't," Imanni said.

Shadae kicked him lightly on the temple. Doriann came around to stand at Imanni's feet. She did not like what Shadae was doing, but she said nothing.

"I'm just an agent," Imanni said. "I deliver writs. I hire others. I'm paid for my work. I don't own your farm."

Shadae just stood there. Surprisingly — he had not expected it — Doriann lowered her hood. Imanni looked at her, gasped, and turned his face away.

"I've been homeless for three years," she said. "Shadae for ten. Maybe, if you had to live on the streets, you'd understand better the evil you've done. Your injuries will heal. My face won't. You'll sleep in a warm bed tonight. I'll sleep under a bridge. I want you to think about that for the rest of your life."

Shadae didn't know whether Doriann was actually able to force that thought on Imanni, but Imanni covered his face with his arm.

Doriann knelt by the butler. "I hope I didn't hurt him too badly," she said. Then she picked up the riverstone she had thrown at him, and stood.

"Now you have two reasons to keep out of the public eye," Shadae said.

"A talent can be hidden," Doriann said.

"Who has the title to my farm?" Shadae asked the man on the floor.

"Tessiar," Imanni said. His voice was muffled by his arm.

"Where can I find him?"

"Her. In Dreystown."

"I can find it. I assume people in Dreystown can tell me where Tessiar is."

"Yes. Everybody knows." He kept his face turned away from Doriann and Shadae as he pushed himself into a sitting position. He supported himself with one hand, and held his neck with the other. "She has talent, too," he said.

Shadae said nothing. Doriann was watching Shadae's face.

"She plays with fire," Imanni went on.

"What does that mean?" Doriann asked Shadae.

But it was Imanni who answered. "She can burn you alive. Slowly. From the inside. Throw fire around like water. Or like stones."

Nobody said anything for a moment. Then the butler moaned. Doriann went to the door, and

Shadae followed her into the foyer, and out of the house, then back the way they had come, toward the inn.

They walked quickly. After a while, Doriann said, "What will you do?"

"I'm not sure. I hope I'll have something figured out by the time I get to Dreystown."

"Is she dangerous?"

"Very. Especially if she can work blind." He was thinking quickly, assimilating all the new information the afternoon had divulged.

"You mean, like, not having to see what she's burning."

"Exactly. But that kind of thing is exceedingly rare."

After a while, Doriann said, "Will you still teach me?"

"If you want to come along. Dreystown is about eight days from here."

"I'm better off with you than by myself," she said.

It did not take long to pack their belongings. Shadae paid the bill, and they left. As soon as they were out of town, a half an hour later, Shadae began helping Doriann discover her talents, her abilities, and her limits. She was smart, and quick. And she was strong. She could move objects almost as big as herself, or small objects at great speed. She could also lift herself up off the ground, just a few inches, and could not carry much more than her clothes. They had few chances for her to read character, and if she had other talents, they would have to be discovered later.

They camped three nights, stayed in a farming

village the fourth, left the road, went through lightly forest country, and camped for the next three nights. There was, after all, a chance that Imanni had been able to send a warning to Tessiar.

It was late afternoon by the time they climbed the last hill. From the top of the bluff, descending steeply before him, Shadae could see the roofs of a small town, or large village, in the forest below. Doriann, beside and a bit behind him said, "I really don't want you to go down there."

He turned to look at her and, as always, seeing her face made him catch his breath, so remarkably ugly, but, by now, strangely appealing. "I know," he said, "but this is what I came to do."

She met his gaze for a moment, then looked out over the forest, not at the town but someplace else. "I just don't want you to get hurt," she said. *Or to die*. She looked back at him. "Do you want me to come with you?"

He hesitated. He did not want her to get hurt either. "Do what you feel you have to do," he said. "If you come with me, you can help me. If you stay here, you can come rescue me, if I don't get back before dark." Or collect his ashes.

She looked down. She did not try to hide her fear, which had been growing as she had learned to use her own talent. "I'll stay here," she said.

"Alright." He stepped off the edge of the bluff, and slid down, inches above the grass, to the forest, and into the trees.

"Wait," he heard her call, and paused so that she, gliding as he had done, could join him.

The Shadow

By Sergey Gerasimov

Darya checked herself in her compact mirror. She puffed out her cheeks, then stuck her tongue in her left one, creating the illusion that everything was OK. It wasn't. The rectangular void threw back a strange image, gauzy like a shadow, with eyes the color of sunshine on the pine bark. She looked for a long moment, struck with a sudden sinking feeling.

She studied World Literature at the university. Now she had Sociology, the most useless subject, after Physical Training, of course. In Sociology, she always took a seat in the last row of desks, liberally decorated with drawings of private parts and explanatory terminology, where, being almost invisible, she could slumber, read her favorite books, or think about the uncharted depths of her latest homework assignment.

Next to her, red-haired Marsha was drawing another railway car on the desk, making the elaborate train a bit longer.

"People need a family to satisfy their natural desires lawfully and to form a social unit," the professor dictated.

"Pardon me, what kind of desires?" red-haired Marsha asked with exaggerated politeness. "I think I've missed something."

"Natural desires," said the professor, looking vain and perfect like Mary Poppins. He pushed up his glasses and droned on.

"Cool. He didn't blush at all," Marsha said. Then she looked at Darya and put her pencil aside.

"What?" Darya asked.

"You look real skinny. Especially in black."

"I use an appetite suppressant spray," Darya lied. "Steady two pounds per week."

It never hurt to give a simple explanation, no matter if it is right or wrong.

"You're a skeleton," Marsha said. "I guess you don't eat at all. You know, when I was fifteen, I was the most anorexic girl in school. I starved myself for days and threw up when I was home alone. I could've even died. But I had control. Everyone wants to have a nice ass."

In the evening, Mother scooped a generous helping of rice on Darya's dish. Mother looked worried. Darya ate all the rice in silence, hating every moment of it. Then she asked for some more.

All the same, Mother decided to call a doctor.

The doctor was a family friend who lived next door. In old times, he had worked with Darya's father. As a friend, he often came over to have mint tea, tell a three-year-old joke, and offer unnecessary advice.

"I see," said the doctor. "How long has she been sick?"

He usually spoke as if Darya were deaf or, at least, far away. Darya sat, looking at the table-cloth, using a small stain as a bench mark. The very blankness of the sight made her feel sad and small.

"I noticed it three days ago," Mother said, exaggerating. "She eats like a bird and never listens to me."

Darya was weighed with the Tanita bathroom scale known for accuracy, unique features, and modern style, which Mother had fished out of the ancient dust under the sofa. Darya had lost twenty-six pounds.

"The scale's wrong," Mother said, "I knew it!"

"Has anything like this ever happened to her before?" the doctor asked.

"Twice," Mother said. "I call it emotional stress. It happens every time she falls for somebody."

And Mother told the doctor about Darya's stresses. About her falling in love for the first time at fifteen, the second time at sixteen, and now at nineteen. These stories were told in detail, as if Darya were deaf or far away.

Darya felt a little ashamed, as if she was hearing and thinking something she should not be hearing or thinking, but Mother was always Mother, and the doctor was a family friend.

"Find something to take her mind off these things," the doctor said. "I'll visit you in a day or two."

That day Darya did not attend her lessons. She was in bed, where the pillow had the same comforting smell she had remembered from the days before emotional stress had yet to mess up her life. The whole day she was eating, reading a book, sipping some vitamin potion and other wonderful concoctions that passed for medicine. She usually did everything she was asked to do. Especially if it agreed with her own wishes.

At dinner, she ate so much rice pudding that she could hardly sit in her chair, and washed it down with a large mug of compote, but an hour later another ten new pounds of her weight disappeared.

"Good heavens, you are as thin as a rake!" Mother said.

Darya imagined herself as the horticultural implement with steel teeth upon which someone was going to step, and the image made her cringe. No, she thought, for goodness's sake, not a rake. I look like a shadow.

Just a few days before, Darya Polsor had been pretty and solid like a young champignon. Now there was nothing left of that, except maybe for prettiness. But even the prettiness had changed; now Darya looked frail like a flower growing in the shade. Only her hair was the same: smooth, with lovely small curls over her ears.

Left alone, she got undressed and examined her new self. She liked her body despite the fact that it lacked the curvaceous geometry she had seen in adult videos. Her breasts were high; her neck flowed with gentle elegance into the supple shoulders; the bones did not stick out. She had not just lost flesh; she became a shadow of herself. She liked being a shadow.

When the sky got dark, she was going out for the evening.

"You'll be at home at eleven," Mother said.

"Mummy, do you know how old I am?"

"Then you're not going at all."

Darya opened her mouth like a surfacing fish. But then, being a right-minded girl, she agreed to the compromise.

The current emotional stress of Darya Polsor was named Stanislas. This Stanislas was a big-framed, clumsy guy who shaved his head bald.

They were walking along the alley of black pyramidal poplars, which stood like solemn ghosts listening to the night wind. The sky was high and full of stars shining desperately through the interlaced twigs as if it were the last night of the world. The air smelled of budding leaves and of last year's hibernating garbage. The lights were off; at the end of the alley, there was a dark arch and a bus stop swarming with sleepily shining buses. Stanislas kept a tedious silence; Darya was tensely silent. She felt uneasy. She watched him with eyes freezing time, imprinting the moment firmly on the pliable velvet of memory.

"Are you going to say a word or two before midnight?" Stanislas said. "I don't even ask for five or six. I feel kinda stupid, you know?"

"What? Oh, sorry. I've been writing an essay on Literature; it's about Thomas Hood. His life, ideas and so on. The deadline is Tuesday, so I've got to hurry. I'm thinking of his words."

"Who was he?"

"'I saw old Autumn in the misty morn stand shadowless like silence, listening to silence,'" Darya quoted, inviting him to talk, pretending not to have heard the colorless tone of his voice. "He wrote that two centuries ago. Isn't it wonderful?"

"It is." His hand slid down her waist. "How long have you been on a diet?"

"You like it?"

"I liked you before, and I like you now. But now you are *too* thin."

"I'm a shadow," she said, lowering her voice.

"Uh-huh," Stanislas answered.

They walked towards the arch. It was early spring; the nights were still cold, but several couples sat on the benches, lurking in the shade. The small shadows sat on the big shadows' laps, for warmth.

"I gotta go," said Stanislas.

She touched his arm. "Why?"

"Getting late." His words were terse.

"No, not yet," her voice was almost pleading, but not quite.

"What difference does it make if you don't say anything interesting? Do you think this is a conversation? You think we're talking? I feel alone. I don't want to be alone. I want to be with you; I want to take you to my place, buy a bottle of something, and turn the light off."

"No, I can't."

"We'd have a really wild time." Stanislas actually looked at her, not exactly imploring her, more of an ultimatum.

"Not now, my mother said-"

"I don't give a shit about your excuses. Seriously. You're provoking me."

He was very near, muscles hard; wooden. "Am I?" The most provocative thing she had ever done was inserting a split infinitive into her creative essay.

Stanislas drew back, said a cold good-bye, and started walking along the alley. Chilled, she watched him moving away from her. He strode confidently. He did not look back.

Darya closed her eyes. "Please, I want to stay with him," she prayed, asking the vast and motionless spectator whose presence shimmered in the air, in the night as clear as a goblet of iced water, who shaped everyone's destiny. "Oh, please, please, pleeease, let me stay with him forever! I want to be his girl, his dream, his wife, his plaything, his shadow, his… "

And something happened. She saw a vertical sky. It moved rhythmically and jerked in time to someone's steps. Darya looked around but could not see herself. Her body was gone. The world had changed: the benches were high; the rail-posts slithered by her very face; Stanislas's back was ahead and above her. The poplars loomed backed by the stars.

I've become a shadow, Darya Polsor thought. *Oh, how fortunate, I've become his shadow.*

A lonely lamppost stood at the arch, illuminating the inside of a fragile green globe of first spring leaves. Darya stretched out across the walk, on the dark uneven asphalt; the ribbed wall of a playground refracted her shoulders and head. Stanislas lit up a cigarette; the small cloud of smoke glimmered in the lamp light. He turned back. A look of mild surprise passed across his face. He shrugged and stepped forward. Darya fell on an advertising board where an exuberant woman, crazy about a brand of yogurt, paraded all her thirty-two, or even a few more, teeth. Being very close to him, Darya could clearly see his face, which looked indifferent now: Stanislas had already forgotten about her.

He threw the cigarette butt away, sniffed at his fingers, cursed quietly, walked through the arch, took a bus. The bus was moving through the night, and Darya, lying on a rubber floor mat, melted into the big shadow beneath the chairs.

Stanislas climbed out of the bus and crossed the street. Darya saw a car speeding to her. The next moment she flew up, slid on the shining metal door, heard a compact burst of music, and fell into the darkness again before she could understand anything.

There was a lamp in the elevator. Stanislas was very tall, but Darya was flat against on the wall at her usual height. Now he was very near. *He's mine,* Darya thought, *from now on I'll be always with him.* She felt especially calm and tender.

At home, Stanislas had supper, and Darya looked at his broad masculine back. A puffy cat, black and orange like a bumblebee, came out of the next room and smelled Darya with evident disbelief. *Shoo!* Darya thought; the cat scratched the floor without enthusiasm, looking half-hearted about the idea, and stretched itself out alongside.

After supper, Stanislas was writing something at the table. A reading-lamp cast his long shadow on the far wall and Darya could not see exactly what he was doing. Suddenly the telephone rang.

"I see," Stanislas said. "At eleven? No, I didn't. I don't remember where. I just said good-bye and… Well, she went somewhere. No, she's not here. Well, that's nice! I don't know."

The telephone rang three times during the night. Stanislas moved drowsily, said something unintelligible or hardly quotable each time, and slammed down the receiver. He did not turn the light on, so Darya was half-asleep. She blended into the general darkness of the room. When the darkness broke away, Darya settled herself on the blue-shadowed silk of the blanket, turning into several dark strips and a small patch at the pillow. Stanislas breathed at her face; she could feel his breathing and the weight of his hand; she inhaled his soothing smell.

At seven, there was a ring at the door, sharp and long. Stanislas sat up on the bed and suddenly moved over. With Darya creeping behind, he went to the front door. Darya touched various things in the room with a housemaker's touch, getting to know everything around, making the things familiar. The gray day was coming through the windows with senseless patterns of distant sounds.

Darya's parents came in. Then came her younger sister -- Darya called her the Splinter -- the doctor, and two police officers. The Splinter looked openly happy to have an excuse to shirk her school lessons.

A policeman strolled round the room, his shoes dirty, his hands in the pockets.

"There, there," he said and looked behind the curtain, evidently inclined to think that it was the best place for hiding the most meaty parts of chopped corpses. The other officer, a woman, sat at the table and prepared to take notes. The bumblebee cat rubbed itself around her legs with the determination of an athlete running laps around the stadium tracks.

"Well, well, well," said the policeman looking into the other room and marking the floor with his footsteps, "the body is not in the apartment."

"I'm alone here," Stanislas said.

The policewoman started writing industriously, with a depressing air of concentration.

"When did you see Darya Polsor for the last time?"

Stanislas answered. He spoke at length and sounded honest. The policeman watched him with a cinematic half-smile.

"So you invited her up here? With you?"

"Well, yes, and she said she had to go home. It was late. Then she left me, just left."

"There are lots of people who saw everything."

"She just left," said Stanislas again.

The people who saw everything were six boys

and twelve girls. Two girls for every boy: the second one was sitting by, just in case, acting as a contraceptive device: spring is a dangerous time. They saw Darya and Stanislas, but nobody could say where Darya had gone. Nobody saw her going out of the park, but everyone saw Stanislas leaving the place alone. Someone saw him smoking, waiting, and taking the bus.

Darya's clothes were found in the morning, and her underclothes were encased perfectly within the outer garments. All the clothes lay precisely arranged, just as if they were laid out in the form of her body. But the body itself had disappeared. There was no blood on the pavement. The police dog could not pick up the trail.

"There's something funny about it," said the policewoman. "Turn the light on."

Stanislas did it. Darya fell on the wall. The policewoman did not look surprised.

"Do you mind if I push all of you out for a few minutes?" she asked. "The victim's mother may stay."

In the next room, the Splinter was examining Stanislas from all directions, trying on her sister's emotional stress. There were curtains on the windows here, and Stanislas switched on the reading-lamp. Darya fell on the door and her left shoulder sank into a chink in it. She could see everything and hear the talk between Mother and the policewoman. However, now the officer turned into an ordinary woman.

"There's no need to worry," she said. "Your daughter just became a shadow. The usual thing."

"But how can you be so sure?" Mother was still clearly distraught, even with such a clear explanation.

"I've seen the shadow of that fool on the wall. She'd been losing weight for days despite all the calories you've been feeding her, right? You've overlooked the beginning of the process."

"Is it dangerous?" Mother asked.

"Not at all. Though, you know, now it's as old-fashioned as wearing a pince-nez. Between you and me, once I turned into a shadow myself. Fifteen years ago. For a short while, for two days."

"And?"

"In a year, he became my husband. He was so-so." The women sighed, rendering homage to the deeper logic of life.

After that, Darya was identified. The policeman brought a table lamp with an extension cord. He placed Stanislas by the wall and lit him at different angles, the lamplight gliding over the brass door-handles and the plexiglas on the desk. Darya was examined closely and recognized. The bosom served as conclusive evidence because Stanislas did not have such a thing. The policeman took a few photographs of this bosom, as material evidence.

"It's not my fault," Stanislas said, "she was always running after me."

"Wow!" said the Splinter, busy with the exciting task of checking out how strongly the cat's tail was attached.

The policeman asked Father and Mother for Darya's picture in the nude. It so happened that they did not have such a picture. "I'm sorry," said the policeman, "but if that's the case we won't be able to make a computer match. We have wonderful techniques, you know. "

That evening Stanislas was invited to Darya's place, to supper. The whole family was there; even the doctor came. Stanislas had flowers. Mother treated him like a suitor. The Splinter dragged along two school-friends and a projection screen. "Let them stay here, please," she said in a voice concentrated like a laser beam, but it did not help: the screen was strung up behind the chair, but the two friends were banished. There was a lamp on the edge of the table. Stanislas was squinting because the light from the lamp blinded him, and Darya was sorry to see that. She was a distinct image on the screen stretched a bit along the x-axis.

Before supper mother asked the doctor to give Darya a check-up, hoping that she had solidified a little. But she had not.

"Maybe, we should feed her?" said mother and put a spoonful of rice to the screen.

But Darya did not want to eat. Especially rice.

The supper dragged on decorously. Everyone except the Splinter was very polite. Stanislas spoke slowly and weighed his words. He evidently wanted to please Father and Mother, and Darya's heart throbbed with joy.

Stanislas went home at ten. Mother took a flashlight to show him to the gate. Stanislas was going away, and Darya was stretching more and more, bifurcated at every street-lamp, hopped on the walls, rushed aside from each car's headlight.

"I think we've forgotten to set the flowers in water," Mother said.

Mother wished to see Stanislas every Thursday; he agreed. He did not buy flowers anymore and

40

tried to leave earlier every evening. A few times red-haired Marsha called him and pumped him for information. Once she came in the flesh, took the reading-lamp in her hand, and looked at Darya. She agreed that Darya did not have a bad figure, but that, of course, it could not be compared to her own nice and slender build.

"Let's check it out?" Stanislas said and gripped her buttock with Neanderthal grace.

"No, not in her presence, she is my friend."

It turned out that Marsha was a true friend, and Darya felt ashamed, because she used to call Marsha 'Marmoset.' But Marmoset was definitely a more suitable name for her than Marsha. Marmoset was what everyone called her behind her back.

At the university Stanislas gathered a gaggle of girls. The girls discussed details of the event and offered advice on personal matters, because they knew that Darya was listening to it. Advice was sometimes complicated, sometimes impudent, whispered in her ear. The dean declared that Darya would be expelled if she did not show up by the spring session.

One day Stanislas did not go to Darya's parents'. Mother called to persuade him. The conversation was long and polite only in the beginning. Stanislas said that he did not want to play suitor anymore. He had had enough of it, there was no love interest at all, he said. Darya listened to him and cried. The shadow shivered on the wall.

He put the lamp behind his back and started to talk. He said quite reasonable words.

"Look," he said. "Isn't that completely psycho? I can't stand it anymore. I'm a man, and that means I have male, er... natural desires. I can't satisfy them because of you. You know, I'm already ready to chase anything with tits. I'm giving you a choice here: you can either turn back into a real woman and stay with me, or I'll call up Marsha to come over, and Marmoset won't refuse. Have no doubt about it."

Darya hesitated. The first choice did not do for a well-bred mother's daughter, but the second was just impossible. In five minutes Stanislas called up Marsha.

Marmoset turned up very quickly, as if she had switched into fast-forward mode.

"Took a taxi," she explained. "Missed you so much. What are we going to do about *her*?"

"About who?" Stanislas had either forgotten about Darya or hoped Marmoset had.

"About this clown, of course," she gestured at Darya, who was still lying on the wall.

"I've tried to make her go, but she doesn't want to. If you can't do it in the presence of your friend..."

"I can't in the presence of my friend, of course, but if she is such a bitch, hehe, she can't be my friend anymore." Marmoset turned to Darya. "Get out of here! He told you he didn't want you anymore. Didn't you?" She turned to Stanislas for confirmation.

"I did," Stanislas lied.

Marmoset gave him her most sugary smile. "So, why is she still here?"

Darya wanted to say something, but only moved on the wall.

"Don't squirm, just go," Marmoset said. "Don't you see you're standing between us?" Marmoset just stared at Darya, saying nothing.

Stanislas came to Marmoset and put his hand on her shoulder. For a short moment, his fingers played in her red hair like wind in a grain field. She turned to him, pulled the lobe of his ear, bent him down, and kissed him, in order to dot the "i"s. Stanislas was very tall. A real man.

"What are we going to do now?" she asked and slumped into an armchair.

"I don't know," Stanislas said, "Frankly, it's killing me."

Marmoset laughed. "It's killing you?" she said. "I hope you have some vodka? It can make a crippled man walk and a blind man see." She sat in the armchair, cross-legged, sexy, shaping the ideas in the air with quick staccato motions of her fingers. "And, you know, just turn the light off."

Darya did not sleep that night. She was invisible and could not see, but the noises she heard spoke to her innocent imagination plainly enough. Some of the noises did not conform to any part of her theoretical grounding in the subject -- which was, after all, as simplified as popular science books. The wall clock sang out two. Stanislas and Marmoset got tired and started cooing about generalities. Darya was crying silently, diffused in the corners. After a while, Marmoset remembered the upcoming session and said that now that Darya had disappeared, there was no one to take good notes in the lectures.

"Darya, are you still here?" she asked.

"She can't talk," Stanislas answered.

"But she can listen. Darya, you must understand. He is not for you. I'm the best woman for him. You're as good a girl as ever could be, too good, in fact. Even in your rear end, there's more IQ than in his frontal lobes. You may hate me if you want, but actually, I'm saving you now. You've got a different destiny. Study, get into science, find a nerd for yourself, and forget Stanislas. He's going to marry me."

"Hey, I never agreed to that!" Stanislas said.

"What did you just say? Dry up, man. I'm not her, understand? If you want to satisfy your natural desires, you must build a social unit. I've heard about it at a lecture."

"And if I don't want to build a social unit?"

"In that case I ring up my father, right now, and he comes here. This issue is closed."

"Closed," Stanislas agreed.

And they again cooed about generalities. When the clock sang out four, Marmoset asked:

"I wonder, is she still there? Let's turn the light on."

She turned it on. Stanislas got out of the bed. The shadow was humbly hanging on the wall.

"This viper has not gone," said Marmoset and cursed in words that would paralyze a rattlesnake, even an insensitive one.

I wish I were a viper, Darya thought, *you'd be dead now.*

"Forget about her," Stanislas said.

"No way!" Marmoset let the blanket slip off the bed. "If she wants to watch, let her see. She will see how a real woman behaves."

"How many guys have you been with?" Stanislas asked and nibbled his lip nervously.

"One," Marmoset said and showed him her middle finger.

"You're a beautiful liar," Stanislas breathed.

"Yes. One, when I was fifteen. I got really drunk and woke up in my friend's house. With my underwear off. And I remember I thought that it was not so important, anyway."

"It was your friend?"

"No, his father." She laughed, then made Stanislas put the lamp on the carpet, so that Darya could see everything. Stanislas turned out to be amazingly obedient.

In the morning Marmoset and Stanislas were cuddling outside. A yellow lamp did not sleep at the drugstore. Darya was lying on the wet strip of bare ground pockmarked by high heels. The rain had stopped an hour before. It was about six: still dark, but the stars were getting pale.

"Do you love me?" Stanislas asked.

Marmoset's eyes glazed for a moment as she thought of the rotten business of falling in love.

"Yep. You think I'd lift up my skirt for anyone? I love you almost as much as your father's Mercedes-Benz."

"Really?"

"Let's close our eyes and count to ten," Marmoset said, "and maybe she'll vanish. It's a good time to go home."

"Listen," Stanislas said. "It's so quiet."

Marmoset listened. It was one of the infrequent moments of real silence around, when the soul feels how something big and important sews seamlessly together the naked edges of yesterday and tomorrow. Small puddles reflected the flamingo-pink edge of the sky. She gave a weary sigh.

"Marmoset," Stanislas said tenderly and kissed her.

"You orangutan!" answered Marmoset with unexpected fury.

They went back home. Darya had gone.

The police visited Stanislas and Marmoset a week later. Two policemen were looking for Darya Polsor again. One of them even produced a picture of the shadow made five weeks before.

For a moment, Marmoset regarded him with a smile no more friendly than a porcupine's back.

"We don't keep company with such uh… dirt," she said, having chosen the right kind of poison. "You can take your photo and go to h- oh, sorry, you know where. I am a soon-to-be-married woman, and Stanislas is my future husband."

She gave Stanislas a resolute smack.

The policemen went about the rooms, marked the floor with their footsteps, looked behind the curtain, but found nothing even there. One of them opened Darya's old notes on literature.

"And I will show you something different from either your shadow at morning striding behind you or your shadow at evening rising to meet you; I will show you fear in a handful of dust. Eliot, 1922," read the officer aloud. "What does it mean? Is it a threat?"

Stanislas creased his face into disciplined furrows. "I don't get it," he said.

So they went empty-handed. Then Darya's father and mother, who had left Splinter at home, came and asked Stanislas to return their daughter. Father even went with Stanislas outside and offered a price. Stanislas did not promise anything.

The fuss lasted about three months. Darya's picture was shown on television. It was a picture from her class-book; in it, Darya Polsor held a carnation and a thick book. She was nice-looking and solid like a young champignon. She was looking down, decently. Then the spring surged, the real spring decorated with the magic sun, exams, and gazes attached to skirts and low-cut blouses. Darya Polsor was expelled. The Splinter shot up and thinned in no time. Mother shoveled rice into her, afraid that the story would repeat itself. But the bony Splinter was not going to turn into a shadow. She put on a most provocative skirt, painted her lips in devilish deep magenta, and started skipping school altogether. The Splinter turned Darya's room into an exclusive club for modern music fans. She wallpapered everything in the house with posters of bands, singers and actors with big guns and biceps.

So Darya Polsor became a dim remembrance of the shadow. Marmoset got married to Stanislas, gave birth to a child, then got divorced, gave the child to her granny and acquired a lover. Stanislas grew a beard and began working at a night club. He wore a uniform and looked quite impressive.

Two years later the doctor was walking along the street of a strange town. He had been late for the bus and now was suffering silently, dragging a heavy bag.

Suddenly he heard quick heels behind, and someone touched his shoulder. He turned back and saw Darya. She was wearing dark glasses and gold ear-rings. She had dyed her hair.

The doctor stared at her in amazement as if he saw a blond nude.

"How do you do?" he asked unable to come up with a better question.

47

"You are always the same," said Darya Polsor and laughed, then became silent and looked very much like the photo from the class-book.

"How's life?" he finally asked.

"Oh, just wonderful. The day before yesterday I came back from Australia. "

"Australia" was an abstract noun for the doctor, similar to "Australopithecus," a word he had learned in the university, thirty-six years prior. He knew theoretically that some people enjoyed distant voyages.

"And what about that boy, Stanislas?" he asked with diffidence, afraid to be impolite.

"Which one?"

"That boy, who..."

"Oh, Stanislas, I forgot. As dead as a dodo. It wasn't serious, in fact. Nothing special."

She took off her sunglasses and met the doctor's gaze. There was not even a shadow of recollection in her eyes; there was just a smile, quick and cold like moonlight dancing in the water of a lake. "How's my family?" she asked, and something in her voice made the doctor feel empty and transient, as if he was watching a flock birds flying over the autumn fields and feeling that the moment will never repeat itself.

"Fine."

"I'll drop in some day. Where are you going?"

"To the bus station." The doctor gestured vaguely toward his destination.

She turned back, waved her hand and a red car slid to the curb.

"Take this man to the bus station," she commanded.

"And you?" the doctor asked?

"I'll walk. I enjoy walking down the street, watching people and all," she answered and took a step off from him.

It was a clear summer morning. The shadows were bright and long. Darya stopped and her shadow stopped too. It was the shadow of a man.

"Darya," called the doctor.

"Aye, what else?"

"Who is it?" The doctor pointed to the shadow.

"This one? Oh, well, some nerd." And off she went, and the shadow stumbled after her.

Passage

by Michelle Herndon

Two figures moved through the night, barely affected by the chilly rain pouring down over their hair and coats. They walked in mutual silence, stepping in the synchronized fashion of men with intent, hands shoved into the deep pockets of their coats.

"Wait," the short one said. "You're telling me you've never read any Hemingway?"

"I don't touch that slop," the other answered, low and gruff.

"Not even 'The Killers?'"

"No."

"You're really missing out, you know. You'd like that one. It's about these two guys—"

"Hush. We're here."

They slowed to a stop and looked to the side as they came near the entrance of a dark alleyway a few blocks down from the mom-and-pop diner from which they had originally emerged. Within its narrow confines, rain water gathered in gutters and on rooftops before spilling down in a single continuous flow, creating muddy puddles in the uneven asphalt upon which crumpled trash floated.

A young man crouched down in the alleyway, sobbing. At his feet rested an equally young woman, once probably attractive, lying on her back between the oily puddles. Her eyes, wide open to the sky, didn't blink to shut out the rain drops that struck her. Her mouth was partially open, but emitted no breath.

"There you are," said the shorter of the two men as they approached the crouched, pathetic form. He looked up, startled, and cringed away from the dark figures that loomed suddenly over him. His mouth opened to speak, but instead let out a strangled, choked-off stutter that meant nothing. A streetlamp nearby glinted off the young man's fangs.

"Uh oh," the shorter of the two continued on, nudging the young woman's body with his boot. She did not move. "Got a little hungry, huh?" He knelt down by the woman's body, and took hold of her chin to tilt her head to one side. There, on her neck, was a deep meaty wound, still covered in fresh blood. "Pretty messy."

"It...it's not what you think!" stammered the young man, trying to scoot away across the pavement. Deeper into the darkness of the alley. "I...I didn't..."

"You didn't what?" snapped the taller of the pair. He stood silently menacing as his companion examined the woman's body.

"I didn't mean to!"

"'Course you didn't," said the shorter, rising from his crouch. He wiped his hands off on his jeans, shrugged a single shoulder. "It's okay, really. These things happen."

The young man's eyes went wide, his struggles to get away faltered, then ceased, forgotten. "W-What?" His voice, barely above a whisper, was drowned by the falling patter of rain.

"The food didn't work, did it?" the shorter of the pair smiled. Even shadowed as it was, his countenance could be construed as friendly. "I can go ahead and tell you now, it never will. Never will again. You can stuff your face with food all you want, drink all the liquid in the world, but it won't ever be enough. You'll still feel that hunger and that thirst. All that food and coffee will get you is an upset stomach later."

"Huh?" The young man shook, eyes darting between the both of them. "I don't know what you're—ugh!"

As though on cue, the young man grabbed his stomach and contorted, moaning, before he turned and emptied his guts onto the ground. Everything he'd eaten in the diner earlier that night came back up, hardly digested.

The taller of the pair frowned hard and wrinkled his nose. "Disgusting."

"There you go," nodded the shorter, his tone properly sympathetic. "Don't worry. You'll feel better in a bit."

The young man groaned, wiping his mouth. "I don't know what's happening," he moaned into a puddle.

"You're a vampire, kid," nodded the shorter. "Plain and simple. But it's my guess you figured that much out by yourself already." He looked down to the woman's body. "What happened? She make a move on you? I tell you, that'll do it every time."

"What are you talking about?" The young man looked up, rain matting his hair dark over his brow. He blinked against it as a slight wind seemed to target his eyes with the rain.

The friendly man smiled. "I told you. It's alright. See? We're like you." There in his grin was a sharp pair of fangs, and as the other, taller figure removed his sunglasses, the young man saw a pair of equally sharp eyes, as red as the blood that pooled around the woman's body. The shorter of the pair crouched back down, bringing himself eye level with the young man. His smile maintained. "My name's Syd. And him, well…he's a card."

The young man was paralyzed by shock and horror, his wide eyes darting back and forth between the two figures. Words abandoned him. Even the sharp prick of his own fangs against his tongue as he opened and closed his mouth couldn't confirm the truth put before his eyes.

Card rolled his eyes skyward with an impatient sigh. "Another mistake. Look at him. Lying there in a puddle like a worm."

"Hey, give him a break," Syd answered over his shoulder. "He's just a kid. Even you had to start out somewhere." He looked back to the young man and extended a gentle hand, palm open . "C'mon. Let's get you cleaned up. We can take care of the body and get you somewhere safe, whuddya say?"

The movement broke him free from the paralysis, and the young man snapped to life, and shrank back. "G-Get away from me!" He smacked the proffered hand away and scrambled to his feet, scraping his hands and knees in an effort to get away. He took off down the alley, running as fast as his wobbly legs could manage. His feet pounded hard on the pavement, splashed through puddles. The rain blinded his eyes.

After only a few feet he smacked hard into something he was sure had not been there the moment before, and fell back onto the harsh alley asphalt. He looked up, blinking his vision back into focus. Card stood over him, towering, with the pale light of a sickly streetlamp at the alley's mouth falling across his features. It might have been the effect of the unnatural light, but his skin was pale white. Unnaturally so. And his expression was fierce.

"Where will you go?" he growled, his voice effortlessly threatening. "Will you keep running?

Diner to diner? Trying to weasel out a pathetic half-existence, pretending to be what you're not?"

"You'll be in real trouble once the sun comes up," came Syd's voice from behind. "Especially if you don't know where to go. Places you think you know aren't as safe as they used to be."

"How long do you think you can ignore that hunger?" Card continued. "You can't win against it. A night, maybe two, before it becomes so great and overpowering you can't help yourself. You'll grab the next person who passes by. It doesn't matter who it is. Stranger or friend, you'll kill to slake that thirst. If you're careless, you'll do it where people can see you." A wolfish grin spread over his face, and that was much more frightening than his scowl had been. "And we can't have that."

The young man's voice hitched in his throat, and he glanced back behind him, beyond Syd, to the limp form of the young woman lying on the ground. "I…I killed her," he whispered, his tone flat.

Card made a sound low in his throat of utter contempt. "Indeed."

The young man lifted his hands to his face and pressed them over his eyes, groaning as he drew his knees up to his chest. He bent his head into them to make himself as small as possible. "I killed her…"

"Like I said," Syd nodded. "It happens. But it doesn't have to. We know people who can help you out. Teach you the ropes. Eventually you can learn not to kill, but still, sometimes you'll slip up. Everyone does."

"Oh God…" the young man started rocking himself, as a child would.

"You're a vampire," spat Card. "By nature you're

a parasite. That's the way things are."

"Oh God, oh God…"

Syd grinned. "Hey, it's not that bad. You won't believe some of the stuff you'll be able to do. Haven't you ever wanted to leap tall buildings in a single bound? Or literally be faster than a speeding bullet? Maybe live forever? Well, live, as a relative term, I mean."

"Oh my God!" the fledgling keened.

The two vampires looked at each other over the young man's hunched and trembling figure, grins fading into shared exasperation. Syd slid a hand into his jeans pocket, pulling out the last of his wrinkled pack of cigarettes.

"Here, then. Have a smoke. Maybe that'll—"

"I killed that girl!" the young man suddenly shouted, lifting his face to the both of them. A man crying out before an altar. "I didn't mean to! Honest! Oh God…what am I? What happened to me?" He rubbed his hands together, and kept rubbing them. "I can't feel my heart. Everything's so cold. I don't want to hurt people!"

"Oh jeez," said Syd, helping himself to the cigarette. "You're not gonna be one of those, are you?"

The young man did not hear him. "I'll never see the sun, ever again! I didn't want this! Oh God…what am I going to do? That's no way to live. This isn't- I can't do this! It's not right! Oh God, what am I?"

Card huffed. "Kids." He reached inside his long coat and drew out a gun, and kept drawing it out. In the end, what appeared was the biggest handgun the young man had ever seen, and its gleaming metal barrel lowered to steady itself right between the young man's eyes. "You won't drink blood? You think this is no way to exist? Very well." There was a metallic click as he drew back the slide. "Allow me to fix that for you."

The young man's eyes were so wide he felt they might vacate his skull. He fell back until his weight rested on his hands behind him, staring and frozen. A rabbit under a hunter's flashlight. His back pressed against Syd's shins, unable to move any further.

"Hey, Card," Syd nodded, with a sound of mild warning. "Ease up, huh? He's just scared."

"Not nearly scared enough," snarled the other in response. "We'll be doing the world a favor by getting rid of another useless bloodsucker. I can't stand vampires these nights! Nothing more than a lot of sniveling teenage goth wannabes feeling sorry for themselves. Useless!"

Syd stepped carefully around the young man and eased forward, reaching out a hand to place on the gun's barrel. He pushed it down, lowering it from the young man's face. "He doesn't know any better."

Card grinned, a flash of fangs in the darkness. "You're right. Look at him. I don't think he realizes just how serious I am."

There was a thunderous, deafening crack as the gun fired, echoing down the alleyway and across city blocks for what could have been miles around. Then there was pain. The most intense, incapacitating pain the young man had ever known. He screamed and grabbed for his leg, pulling it close to him as though that would alleviate the agony. Blood trickled from the gaping wound that tore all the way through his pant leg and out the other side, darkening one of the puddles the young man sat in.

His entire frame shook, eyes clenched shut, biting his lip hard in an attempt to keep from crying out any more than he already had. Still he whimpered, and felt the burn of tears in his eyes.

"Hey!" Syd snapped, and shoved Card away from the sniveling newbie. "What's wrong with you?"

Card snarled, baring his fangs. "I'm teaching him a lesson! That's what we're here for, am I right?"

"Not like that, you crazy git!"

"And why not?" Card lifted his gun again, but Syd caught his arm in a lock with both of his own, placing himself between the shooter and the young man cowering on the ground. Card kept his eyes on the whimpering wounded topic of conversation. "He doesn't want to live like this. He said so himself. We can grant his wish." Card began to level the gun at the boy's head again.

"You've overstepped yourself this time, mate," Syd growled, flashing his own teeth in reply as an accent previously hidden deep in his voice rose closer to the surface. "You can't do this."

"And who's going to stop me? You?"

"Damned skippy."

The young man heard a struggle, but could not see it all entirely, distracted as he was by the pain in his leg. They both moved so fast. Both of them could have stepped into the same puddle and been gone before the first ripples even reached the water's edge. He heard grunts of effort and bestial snarls, and finally one of the pair slammed back against the alley wall. Hard. The young man saw the brick and cement buckle in from the impact, and a dark figure slumped down to the ground, motionless. He blinked. It was Syd.

Slowly the young man's eyes lifted back up to

the vampire who remained standing. The one with the gun. Though it no longer beat, he felt his heart sink as burning crimson eyes turned to focus on him. That grin — absolutely manic — released a low, throaty chuckle.

"Now, where were we?"

Card stalked slowly toward the young man, taking his gentle time. The young man gasped, tried to scramble away, but putting any weight on his injured leg was out of the question. When he looked up again, the gun was back in his face.

"Normally the likes of us aren't affected by bullets much," said Card, smug. "But the ones in this gun are something special."

The young man whimpered, casting a glance beyond Card's image to where Syd's form still lay slumped against the wall. Silently he wished the figure back to life. To protect him.

"P-P-Please!"

"What?" snapped the vampire. "Are you going to beg now? I expected as much."

The young man ducked his head so that his chin pressed against his chest, closing his eyes tight. He heard his own voice, rasping, pathetically small. "Please..."

"Please what? Speak up, wretch!"

"P-Please! Don't kill me!"

Card laughed, and it was the sound of a dead stick being dragged along an iron grate. Pointed scorn and disdain, but no real life. "And why shouldn't I?"

Whimpering, the young man could not think of an answer. He felt the cold metal gun barrel press to his forehead.

"Don't worry," Card hissed. "I'm doing you a

favor. Being killed this way is much less painful than being staked and left out for the sunrise, or torn apart by your fellow monsters. Oh, and I'm sorry about the bullet in your leg." The lilt in his voice suggested anything but. "Does it hurt?"

Sobbing, the young man nodded. The gun's barrel bobbed with the movement.

"Poor little fledgling. Allow me to put you out of your misery."

"Wait…"

The young man's voice was small and fragile, but it was enough to momentarily pause the vampire's finger from clenching around the trigger.

"Please…"

"What?" Card huffed. "More begging? It's only amusing for so long, wretch."

"Please don't kill me."

"Why?"

"Because…I…"

"Because what, wretch?" Card snarled, and pressed the gun harder against the young man's skull.

"Because, I…"

"Speak up!"

"Because I want to live!" The young man blurted, and the dam was broken, the cries he had been holding back flooded his existence. His shoulders jerked and his body shook with the sobs that reverberated through him. Tears, bright crimson, escaped his eyes to creep down his cheeks and stain his shirt collar, only to be diluted by the incessant rain. "Please! I want to live! I don't want to die!"

"And why do you want to live?" the vampire snarled, pressing the gun down again for emphasis.

"You're wounded and in pain. Just a moment ago you were expressing a wish to die. Why change your mind now?"

"B-Because…that will change! I can change! I want to live…tomorrow will be different…"

There was silence in the alleyway, save for the continual patter of rain that tumbled from the cloudy sky above. For a long moment, nothing moved. The young man sat curled and cowed in a puddle of bloody mud water. The vampire stood over him, gun pressed to the young man's forehead, waiting with the certainty of a trained and practiced executioner.

At last, several lifetimes later, the gun lowered and Card grunted, "Very well."

The young man's eyes snapped open. Disbelieving, he looked up, slow and tentative, lest it be a ruse to get him to drop his guard. But Card's expression was blank as he slid the gun back beneath his coat. Behind him, against the wall, Syd sat up and climbed to his feet.

"I knew you didn't mean it," said Syd, grinning, as he approached and offered a hand to help the young man up. "Welcome to the freaky little family, son."

Numbly, the young man watched his hand respond of its own volition, taking the proffered grip, strong as steel, that lifted him to stand like he was nothing. Syd's other hand produced a small folded piece of paper.

"Here," he said. "That's the address for a church just outside of town. A friend of mine runs it. Just head over there and say we sent you and he'll fix you right up. Might even take care of that wound for you." He grinned and winked, lifting a fresh cigarette to his mouth. "Don't worry about the crosses or anything. They probably won't hurt you."

Though his mouth worked to say something, no words came from the effort. The young man took the slip of paper between numb fingers and pushed it into his pants pocket. He looked between the two faces before him, one nodding in affirmation, the other coldly replacing his sunglasses over his eyes. Neither of them said a word. Then he turned, the pain of his wound somehow lessened, and limped away down the length of the alley. After a few moments, he disappeared into the night and the rain.

"That was fun," the slightly shorter of the pair lingering in the alleyway grinned. "But did you really have to shoot him?"

"He looked like he needed the added motivation." Card reached inside his coat and withdrew the gun, holding it by the barrel a moment to observe it from behind the emotionless black of his sunglasses. With a disdainful huff, he handed it over to Syd. "Here."

Syd reached out to take it, blowing off imaginary dirt and polishing the metal quickly with one sleeve. "Maybe next time you should get thrown up against the wall." He held the gun and eyed along the barrel.

"I barely pushed you." Card reached to adjust the red scarf around his neck as he turned, heading down the alley in the opposite direction of the young man.

Syd followed, snapping the revolver shut after examining the leftover bullets and tucking it away inside his coat. He glanced to the indention left in the brick wall as they passed it. "Uh huh." He sighed, letting his shoulders sag. "Guess that's what I get for being such a nice guy."

"Yes. It is."

Syd chuckled. "Anyway, 'The Killers,' right? It's this story about these two guys who go into a diner…"

Drucy's Tale
A Tale of *The Scorched Earth*
by Kenneth Gentile

Drace cracked an angry gray eye open at the beam of rising sun shining through the shamblewood shutters. "Burning Eye," he muttered under his breath as he eased the joygirl's arm off of him, mindful of the needle-like claws slightly protruding from the aelf's fingertips. As he sat up on the end of the rack-like bed, a quick touch showed him his coin pouch was still secured between the mattress and the rope-slats that supported it, unpilfered during the too-short sleep. He got up, the ache of his knee starting anew, and gave a soft pat on her thigh to rouse her, the light sheen of tawny fur tickling his rough palm. Hobbling over to dresser, he grabbed a toothrag from his kit and went to cleaning the sleep from his mouth, swishing a small shot of travel-ale around to kill the rather furry trail-rat which had apparently nested there while he slept.

"You knows, you can gets that hobby knee fixed here, sirrah." The joygirl yawned from the bedrack "I knows the Brother Medico that comes here. He'll do you up good and gives you a good price fer yer coin."

Drace glanced into the shard of mirror remaining in the frame of the roughly used dresser, and then lifted his tabard from the scarred dresser top, showing her the symbol upon it, an ebon crow on a disc of brass splotched by russet smears, and went back to cleaning his teeth.

The girl coughed a bit "Ah, I sees, sirrah, pardon."

Drace caught the wrinkling of her flat up-turned nose and the way she pulled the threadbare blanket up to her a bit more, a linen shield against the "boogey stories" she'd been told between tricks as a child.

"Sirrah, not be bother to you, but it's time I be leaving if you've had your worth of me."

Drace shrugged, feigning ignorance. In the glass shard, the joygirl squirmed a bit as she lifted her silks and bells from the floor and hastily covered herself with them. Drace made a show of checking his teeth, buffing the short brutal-looking canine "tusks" that extended from his bottom jaw, leftovers from the Old Kingdoms and the founding of his species.

The aelf started, and Drace's keen ears picked up the slight gulp from her throat.

"Well, sirrah... there's the... er... payment, sirrah." Drace stopped, looking at the girl in the mirror, and raised a dark eyebrow in question.

"Payment?" he replied, his voice a rough growl, much rougher than his normal pitch.

The girl looked pale, even through her slight sheen of fur, her pupils wide in the dim room, almost overcoming her jade irises completely. Even though the room was warming quickly in the morning sun, it was not nearly enough for the scent of sweat beginning to emanate from the bedrack. "Yes, sirrah, we... arranged a payment for the night? I should get that now, if it's not too much bother."

Drace turned and leaned back on the dresser, his thick forearms crossed over his broad, equally scarred chest. "Payment? Was there a payment agreed upon?" Drace locked the joygirl with a hard-steel eye, his face a deadly serious.

The fidgeting became more intense, the girl standing and moving ever so slowly for the door, her finger-tip and toe-tip claws extending and retracting in an instinctual response forged hundreds of years in the past. Although not nearly as vicious as old texts recorded her forbearer's as being, more than one modern-day roughneck had found out the hard way that although small, they were sharp as razors and the venom, though diluted through the ages passed, was still painfully endowed. "Yes, Sirrah... if you please... you said a ring-silver for pleasuring and a second if I stayed with you 'til you rose."

Drace chuckled for a second. Two ring-silvers was half a joygirl's rate in towns as small Ridgeback or Hazeville, and quite a bargain against rates he'd find in Browder's Bridge or the Copperhail. But for a crossroads travelers' rest like this, it was pretty much standard. Yet, the girl had thought it a fortune the night before. It made Drace wonder if she was really as young as she appeared.

"Two rings, was it?" Drace pinched and pruned his thick brown goatee, as if pondering the concept. "Quite a price, girl. Do you think you earned it?"

Shock crossed her face and Drace knew at that moment. Any joygirl with experience would've crowned him with his own mace for a comment like that. "Um, Sirrah. If that was too much, I would settle for one."

Drace could not restrain himself any longer, and the girl looked as though she would faint dead away as he suddenly burst into laughter.

"By the Broken One, girl! I'm teasing you. You'll have your two rings. And I'll add a breakfast that'll make you waddle childbirth-like if you'll answer a few questions true and clear. Is it a deal, girl?"

The girl, slightly stunned by the sudden change of the man's demeanor, sat on the bedrack.

Drace regarded her for a moment. "What's your name girl? And don't tell me it's 'Drucilla o' the Wynd' either. Your *real* name, if you please."

The girl looked at her toes for a moment. "Well, sirrah. It is Drucilla, sirrah. I just added the rest. They... they call me Drucy, though, sirrah."

"Drucy's a fine name, girl. You don't have to add all that flowery dung. Hellstouch, a girl as pretty as you could call yourself 'Dusthollerer' and still have the soldiery lining up around the bar to give you their wages for a kiss-n-cuddle." Drace watched as the girl lit up for a moment, then seemed to catch herself, divining the meaning of his words.

"You know how to braid, Drucy?" The girl nodded, and Drace sat with his back to her, flipping his long hair back. "Make it close to the base of my head, and keep the braid tight." As Drucy began to braid the thick coarse brown hair, Drace pushed his inquiry. "Not your plan to be a joygirl, is it Drucy?"

"Oh, yes, sirrah-" she began, but Drace interrupted.

"You promised me the truth, Drucy."

The girl swallowed. "No, sirrah."

Drace pinched at his goatee. "I see. Crops not good this time of year, are they?" The girl continued braiding, careful not to pull Drace's shaggy mane too hard. "No, sirrah. The winter rains weren't good enough, so the sow grass is barely enough to keep the cowks, and with the cost of the hardyseed almost doubled by the Agroshold... well, one of us had to go, and with my parents dead this 15 seasons, my uncle sold me."

"Ah." Drace nodded slightly. "Flesh-Trader, I

suppose?"

The girl clasped his hair with the leather collar, confused by its odd shape. "Sirrah, I'm not sure how this goes?"

Drace took the braid and wrapped it around his throat like a torc, then clipped the end with the hard leather sheath. "Keeps it out of the way, but pulls loose quick in a fight if someone grabs for it. Now, how did you end up here?"

"Well, Baintis—he was a nomesh—he turned out to be a good sort, sirrah. Never tried to touch me or beat me. Actually, seemed to take a shining to me. Turn out he had a load of Hobbled Owing that he needed help feedin' and such, so he put me to task and in exchange never offered me to the block. He never said, but I think theys was meant for the Weblands. Anyways, when wes got to Donstown, he found me a fella and dowered me off to marry him, instead of me going to the Bloodspiders." The girl shuddered visibly at the mention of the arachnea. Drace had fought against their soldiers many times, strange and sadistic creatures laughingly referred to as "men." Not a good fate for anyone to find their way there, especially a young girl like Drucy.

"Then Edding, he got different as soon as Baintis was over the horizon and we were at his home. Turned out he had several girls and they, well they were all joygirls, sirrah. We used to talk at night while he was out drinking, turned out all of thems was bought the same way."

Drace looked at her wrists, where several cheap bell-bangles hung. "So, how much you owe him? I don't see your buybangle?"

Drucy looked up at him, confused. "Buybangle,

sirrah?"

Drace blew out his breath hard through his broad flat nose. "I think you've earned your rings, Drucy." He forced a smile.

The girl smiled back, "And the breakfast?"

Drace nodded, pulling on his tunic and belting it, then retrieving his purse from the underside of the bed. He glanced over at the thick-hafted iron mace, but decided in his mood, that would only lead to trouble. Opening the door, he looked down at the snoozing stable boy that lay across the doorway. A tap of his booted foot brought the boy wide awake. "Morning, Sirrah!"

Drace nodded. "No visitors last night, lad?"

"None, sirrah," the boy replied. "Slept like a baby, I did."

Drace chuckled, and reached into his purse extracting a ring-silver. The boy's eyes lit up like ghostlights in a cave fisher's orbs. "Now, I promised you a half-ring. You want the other half as well, boy?" The boy nodded with such vigor, Drace though he would hurt himself. "Then this is what I want you to do: you guard my room, and keep near the window. When I'm ready to leave, I want you to bring down my stuff to me. Deal?"

"Yes, sirrah!" The boy hopped to his feet and stepped into the room, and Drace stopped him with a firm arm.

"You get a friend to help you guard, and tell him there's a half-ring in it for him as well, when the deal is done. Okay?" The boy nodded again. "Good. And don't go through anything. You know what I am, boy; I carry daemons in my pockets that might enjoy a snack of a young boy's misguided fingers, you hear?"

With that he handed over the silver ring to the stableboy, who fit it over two fingers to keep it safe. Many townships and kingdoms had their own currencies, but rings, bracelets, and torcs were commonly accepted, different sizes and metals but approximately the same weights, forged and marked with the Woldbanc stamp. Relatively safe from counterfeiting or "scraping" for fear the Auditors would catch word. Utterly ruthless, Woldbanc's assassins had a reputation of "taking their measure," usually paid in flesh and bone. Literally.

Knowing his possessions would be secure, Drace led Drucy down the steep stairs to the main hall of the rest, and to breakfast.

Eddings's black eyes never drifted far from the patrons coming in and out, the distance to his ale mug and no farther. Normally, daybreak would not have been so popular, and he would have stayed in town in his bed and the arms of one of his girls until after midday, but last night word got to him that Tyson's Black Banners had come in late in the night.

The Banners were a mercenary unit, 200 men strong, not counting camp followers and recruits, and the rumor was they pulled wagons loaded with spoils from the last six months of posting in Durleigh Township, securing their southern borders from the Lantian Cities' raiders. Instead of pushing for the hills toward Tyson's Blackhold, they chose to meet their paymasters here, to trade goods and recruit replacements before returning to the hold for spring and their shift as a brigade in service to the City-State of Usher in the highheats of summer.

They set in at Martinette Lak Crossing, the last travelers' rest along the Forty before the hills began in earnest, which meant quite a few soldiers bored and moneyed, and with much more time than any camp joygirl could rightly handle. His mind whirled at the figures, with a ring per girl per two hours, he could buy his way into the Townships with a small title and live the highlife by the end of the week.

Of course, that meant keeping the lazy sows moving, of course. Three had not been seen in over four hours and Drucilla, the newest, had not been seen since last night. Eddings wished he had found the time to break her properly, but he could not lose one bedhopper from this veritable treasure-trove of wealth. Even Truneese, his nomesh girl, had been funneling rings and stones to him all evening and into the wee hours, the blood-soldiers not picky about their bedmates. One thing he cursed himself for was that a number of Tyson's Black Banners were female, with a preference clearly lacking in his stable. He was becoming sorely tempted to rent himself out for a bit of coin, but he needed to be here to prevent the few independent joygirls from working *his* customers.

His musing over, Eddings's eyes scanned the room, and spotted his wayward girl, sitting with a brute of an aelforix... and *laughing?* Eddings began to seethe as he watched the aelf bitch, sitting like a Highdowns Duchess, fawning over the soldier and eating like a pig. He looked over the man quickly, noticing no sign of the Tyson's sigil, a black mountain on white background, which the Black Banners wore so proudly. More than likely a recruit, not yet trained, or a solo looking for handouts from a professional group like Tyson's. *Good*, he thought to himself, *no affiliation, no protection*. He stood, stretching his two-yard-and-two frame, keeping his hand on the heavy brasswood Tyrstester club hanging from his belt. Many a man in Donstown and the surrounding villages could attest to the skill and steadiness of his hand, even when he was a bit in the wind, as he was now. With a sneer to the barmaster, he strode purposefully toward Drucy's table, popping the tabletop with a loud rap of the knobby cudgel.

"Here now, what a nice feast, you have m'lady!" he said as he plopped down, helping himself to a chunk of cheese, from the platter in front of the pair, "Mind if I join you?"

"Eddings, I was just finishing up!" Drucy stammered out, "I was almost done, but the Sirrah here, he asked me to breakfast with him." Eddings cast a cruel glance from Drucy to Drace and back again. "L-look," she continued, holding out the twin rings in her palm "He paid me, he did, double too, and bought the breakfast!"

Eddings snatched for the rings, pulling his hand back to feel nothing in his palm. The aelforix looked down at his own hand and opened it, the two ring-silvers glittering in his palm, which he promptly gave back to Drucy. Eddings glared his meanest look. "Am I going to have trouble with you, doggy?" he made another rap with the cudgel on the table to emphasize that he was not the man to have trouble with.

Drace sighed, and gently closed Drucy's fingers around the rings. "I paid *you* for the night, not him. These are *yours* to keep." With that, he popped another chunk of meat into his mouth, and continued dining as if Eddings were not looming over the table. By now, several of the surrounding tables were paying some attention to the encounter, grins breaking across several of the mercenaries' faces. Drucy shrank into Drace's side as Eddings's face began to redden. Drace raised his mug, but it never met his lips as Eddings snatched it out of his hand and slammed it down on the table.

"You," he glared at Drucy, "to my table now! I'll deal with you in a moment." He turned to Drace, who was completely ignoring him. Drace put his hand on Drucy's shoulder and guided her back down to her seat.

"He doesn't own you, Drucy." The man said, his voice as even as a sword blade. "Bought joygirls receive what's called a buybangle from their Fleshseller when they're purchased like you were. It indicates how much you owe the buyer. Once it's paid off, any honest pimp cuts the bangle free, and word is sent to the Fleshseller. At that point you can go as you please, or renegotiate your deal with the pimp. You don't have one, which means Baintis truly believed the price he was paid was a dowry for marriage." He looked at Eddings, who was now crimson faced and puffing, "and *not* for whoring. I'm willing to wager that none of the girls working for Eddings has one. Which means that when I leave here, I'm going to put the word to the next Fleshseller I see that he's a thief and get him blacked. That goes to the Skinguilds, and your *master* here won't get so much as a whiff of another deal. No Skinguilder, be it seller, joygirl or boy, pimp, or even harvester will ever deal with him again."

Eddings looked as though he was going to explode and began to sputter out a threat when Drace raised a hand.

"And, if he's smart, he'll realize that he's very

lucky that I don't step outside and put the word to the wagon masters as well, or there'll be some very angry mercenaries in here, asking to see his Skinguild brand." Drace smiled. "In any case, you don't owe him anything. My advice would be that after you finish you fill of breakfast – as was our deal – that you decide where you want to go next. I'm sure the barmaster would be happy to have a pretty girl like you to be a joygirl here, or even to work as a serving girl if you wish."

"Or you could step outside and talk to the wagon-masters. I'm sure they could guide you to any number of camp madams that would be happy to have you work with them. Mercenaries are hard, but well-paid, and they treat their camp joygirls with quite a bit of care and respect. You might even entice one of them into taking you as his mistress or wife."

A rousing shout of offers and approval from several of the mercenaries currently eating and drinking in the hall reinforced his suggestion. "Although I don't recommend you marry one of these lecherous thugs, because invariably the wives find themselves as the cuckolds to the former. Best you start at the *top* of the food chain," Drace added loudly, which brought a round of laughter from the hard sell-swords, each playfully, if roughly, admonishing each other about their faults in the area of fidelity.

"But in any case, from this point on, your life is your own. Do with it what you will." Drace turned to face Eddings who was angrily tapping his cudgel into his free hand. "But so there's no confusion. I will say it very slowly: You. Don't. Own. Her. So. Go. Away." Finished, Drace took a deep drink from his mug, completely ignoring Eddings again.

Off sides, a mercenary with one eye missing and a gray beard hanging to his waist, obviously at least partially dawarvek in breeding, leaned to his companion, a massive bald man easily two-and-six dressed in a black sleeveless chain-and-tunic and leather braces. "Stupid for a half ring-gold, what say ye, Gild Jyantborne?" The huge merc loosed a thundercrack boom of laughter, tugging on his own long beard, braided in three long plaits.

"No wager, Vise. It would be fool's gold in your purse, and you'll have none from me."

Eddings's eyes bulged as the laughter rang around him. He had to save face, and if that meant crushing this brute's thick skull, then that is what he would do. The cudgel whistled through the air in a horizontal arc with enough force to take the aelforix's head clean off his shoulders until it stopped dead in Drace's hand. The aelforix's face broke into a wide grin, half-tusks gleaming in the morning sun and ghostlight.

"Stupid," both Vise Stilloneeye and Gild Jyantborne said in unison, and broke into deep laughter.

Eddings hit the hardpack ground in a shower of shamblewood splinters, more than a few of which were still buried in his prone form. He would have yelled in pain, but the two halves of his jaw simply would not work together, so it came out as a spray of blood and broken teeth. He rolled over, trying to stagger to his feet, half of his broken cudgel still hanging by the thong at his wrist. From the window through which he had just made his assisted egress, he could see money changing hands as bets were placed, not on the winner, but on the extent of the beating he was about to receive. He spun, only to see a wide span of knuckles entering his vision at high speed.

Then the sun grew suddenly dark, and the ground shifted from beneath his feet. Funny, he could not recall an earthquake in this area before. Suddenly he was upright again and looking into the eyes of a daemon. Eddings did what any man would at that point, and fainted dead away.

Drace accepted the rag from Vise, and wiped the blood from his face.

"I'm gonna have to reset that again. Now or later?"

Drace steeled himself and nodded, the dawarvek chirurgeon grabbed his nose and pulled sideways with a loud "pop." The world swam and grew dim for a moment, but Drace found himself supported by the short rock called Vise. "The girl?" he asked.

Vise gestured, and through watery eyes Drace could make out the form of Drucy standing in the doorway, the protective hand of Gild Jyantborne enveloping the girl's shoulder. "Unharmed and safer in Gild's hands that in her mother's womb, I reckon." Vise popped him in the nose with a blunt finger. "Oh, yer a jackalope's arse, Drace Wynterborne" he said matter-of-factly, and strolled away.

Drace stumbled over and sat on the stairs, and Drucy began fawning over him with a wet rag.

Gild just chuckled and shook his head. "Leave him be, and gather up your things and your friends, little willow. Old Gild'll look over you until you're done." The aelfjyant looked down. "Will you be alright, Brother Drace?"

Drace nodded. "I will. There are some boys in my room, care to tell them to fetch my things for me?"

Gild chuckled, "Done and done, Brother."

As the boys arrived, bundles in tow, they both halted at the sight of the small pile of rings, bracelets and stones that formed at Drace's feet. "Sirrah?" One began to ask.

"My fair tithe, lads. They were betting on me, and this is my share of the winnings. Keep an eye on it for a moment?" The boys nodded, and Drace began to put his gear on.

He exchanged slippers for knee-length boots of oiled crowk leather, and over his homespun tunic and breeches, he dropped a gray steel scale-and-leather jerkin that draped from neck to knees. Pauldrons of steel were strapped over each shoulder and upper arm, and matching greaves over either shin. The armor was well kept but battered in places, as if the battle scars were left with purpose, and the armor repaired just enough to maintain integrity. Wide plate had been lacquered in shining black, and trimmed with steel, and the black scales bore the resemblance of the feathers of a crow or raven. A sleeveless robe — the item Drucy had thought to be a tabard — of dark gray and black, was hung over the armor like the vestments of a cloister, giving Drace an almost priestly look about him as he drew on the blackened steel gauntlets.

Finally, a simple helm, also of steel and black lacquer with a half-coif of black scale hanging from the edges of the helm, was seated on his head, and he gingerly adjusted to the nose guard to ensure it did not bother his broken nose too much. The boys almost reverently handed him his heavy mace, and its hammer twin, as they realized what they had served unknowingly. About his neck, he hung the symbol of his rank and faith, the ebon crow on a disc of brass, dried smears of the "Blood of Contracts" still there, some of the stains a decade old, each representing a contract between a mercenary company such as Tyson's and the contractor, each bound in the eyes of his faith.

Eddings looked up from his resting place as Drace turned. "Stormsbreath! A Crowpriest. I attacked a hellsdamned Crowpriest!"

Drace grinned and gestured at the black steel spurs on his boots, and Eddings fainted dead away again.

"A hellsdamned Paladin of Corvas, actually," he chuckled, as a crow cawed from some battlefield distant.

Waiting for him to arrive.

The Observatory Gardens

by James McCarthy

The professor woke up earlier than usual this morning. His little dog was barking at a neighbor's cat just outside the window. As he gently scolded the dog, he looked out of the window and noticed that a light snow had fallen during the night. A few tiny flakes still danced slowly to the ground.

Deciding on coffee rather than tea, he drank it leisurely, and dressed in his customary twentieth century style suit and coat.

He was fascinated by Old Earth history and culture, particularly the late nineteenth and twentieth century. Neither was he alone in his interest. Many of the buildings in neighbouring Cambridge were influenced by Victorian style architecture to some degree.

He walked out into his yard, perfectly comfortable in his long heavy coat with its warm secure hood. With a small smile he felt a stab of delight as he watched the sunrise, its light glistening as tiny sparkles scattered on the soft violet hues of the new fallen snow.

"How excruciatingly pleasant," he always liked to say to himself during times like this.

For the professor had always made it a point to never take the beauty of simple everyday nature for granted.

He thought of himself as a bit like Mole from *The Wind in the Willows*, for he, too, was but a simple animal of tilled field and hedge-row, linked to the-

A luminorph!

It was a small glowing pale blue-green blob in the distance, slowly drifting through the air. It was heading in his direction and soon it entered his yard, hovering a few feet off the ground.

It was a small luminorph, about a foot long and jellyfish-like in appearance, though even more amorphous.

The professor realized how lucky he was that morning. Sunrise and snow was one thing, but a luminorph sighting in winter was rare.

Now, Validon in spring, that was altogether different. Validon was the province in which professor lived. In April (for the months on the world of New Terra had been named after the months back on Old Earth), luminorphs in all shapes, sizes and species were a fairly common sight in the country, especially after the rain. They would rise up from shallow water to float through the sky, or slowly creep across the meadows, seeking shelter among the caves and ruins.

New Terra, somewhat smaller than the Old Earth, also was located in the suburbs of the Milky Way Galaxy, yet was much less crowded. It was a best-kept secret, an out of the way little place in the country (astronomically speaking) in a more remote part of the galaxy.

It was one-hundred years ago when the luminorphs were first spotted near ancient but well known ruins back on Old Earth. People had approached the luminorphs and were ultimately led to the portals which opened up among the ancient ruins: trans-dimensional portals through which one could walk from that world into this one, the world of New Terra. Although the locals still called it "Rahir."

Needless to say, that had changed everything. It

was through these portals that the early twenty-first century citizens of Old Earth were able to colonize New Terra and other worlds.

The existence of the luminorphs had been at first doubted as a hoax until their population increased and sightings became more numerous in and around the ancient places of Old Earth. The first reported encounters came from farmers and tourists near Stonehenge in England, just a handful of luminorphs. A month later, there were a dozen or so, either floating through the air or creeping along the countryside near the ancient stone structure. The news media and thousands of others began to flock to the scene.

Those first luminorphs were translucent and amorphous. They were brightly glowing, multicolored entities that resembled jellyfish, some tiny, some quite large, which eerily floated through the air around the circle of stones like ghostly spirits.

Other, more solid luminorphs, which also resembled jellyfish or cephalopods and weird tropical plants or trees, began to appear. They floated slowly through the air, closer to the ground. They would almost lazily guide themselves along with branch-like tendrils, lightly touching, then pushing off from the ground beneath them in a sort of half-walking, half-swimming manner, like a person walking in water just over their head.

Later another group of these plant-like luminorphs appeared. They resembled fungi, sponges or small strange trees covered in vines and walked or crept along the ground at a snail's pace. From a distance, one could scarcely perceive them as moving. They glowed less frequently and much more subtly than the other luminorphs as they made their way along the fields nearby, never taking to the air as the others did.

Soon, there were luminorph sightings in six other places around the world: among the fig tree covered ruins of the ancient temple-city of Angkor Wat in Cambodia; outside the Great Pyramid of Giza in Egypt; by the ruins of Chaco Canyon in New Mexico; Chichen Itza in the Yucatan peninsula; Machu Picchu in the mountains of Peru; and the oldest ancient observatory in Gaocheng, China.

At first, the luminorphs were met with some fear and trepidation. Where did they come from, and how did they get here? Was it the precursor to an alien invasion? A sign of the Apocalypse? Why did the luminorphs suddenly inhabit these various ancient sites?

After awhile, people became less fearful around the luminorphs as the strange but beautiful creatures seemed to pose no threat. They showed no signs of aggression as they went about their way, paying little heed to gawking onlookers.

When people inevitably came into physical contact with the luminorphs, reactions varied. Those who touched the plant luminorphs felt only a dull warmth and moist tactile feeling no different than touching any other ordinary plant. However, when a person could reach out to touch one of the larger air-born translucent luminorphs, they would experience a slight sting like a mild electrical shock. This would often be followed by a mild sense of euphoria and a feeling of insight. This sense of insight was generally a vague notion that something strange and wonderful was about to happen in the not too distant future. Others claimed that when they touched these luminorphs they sensed a definite wise old intelligence in them, even a sort of telepathic link, as well.

Scientists and others tried to capture some of the luminorphs out of scientific curiosity or for politically and financially motivated reasons, but this proved to be impossible. It was as if the luminorphs could tell what these people were trying to do and would quickly dart away like a frightened cuttlefish (which some of them resembled), suddenly blinking off and on, strobe-like, dazzlingly bright, temporarily blinding their would-be captors.

The ground-dwelling plant luminorphs were easy to hold onto of course, but if someone tried to make off with one, a group of small glowing translucent luminorphs would appear out of nowhere (literally) and surround the plant luminorph. Then it, along with the other luminorphs, would all simply disappear.

It only added to the mystery that these remarkable creatures actually had the ability to simply reappear and disappear, even in broad daylight. People would try to grab onto them, only to have them vanish in their hands. These luminorphs did not simply become invisible, for their warmth would no longer be felt in one's grasp. They suddenly and simply were no longer there. Yet you could often see that same luminorph reappear at that same moment, twenty meters away from you, blinking in an agitated state. It was as if, like an electron, they could instantly leave our dimension, travel to another and return instantly.

It was a month after the luminorph phenomena had "gone global" when the first trans-dimensional portal materialized at Stonehenge. It was around midnight, but there were still plenty of tourists, self-styled pilgrims, reporters and other people milling around. They were witnesses to the first event. The portal appeared between two of the standing stones, first as a dull misty green glow that almost went unnoticed, except by one little girl and several stoned hippies. The mist soon became bright and multicolored.

"Look!" someone shouted, and people one by one turned their gaze in that direction. Soon a different landscape appeared between the stones, like looking through a doorway.

Naturally, the first to enter the portal were the stoned hippies, who did so without hesitation and against the stunned and terrified admonition of their fellow witnesses. They returned immediately, telling everyone that from their perspective, they had been gone for several minutes, hours, days, maybe longer. They told tales of the strange and amazing places where they had been, most seemed to be visiting one planet in particular.

Shortly after, portals simultaneously opened up at the six other ancient sites around the world where the luminorphs had appeared just a few weeks earlier. The Great Pyramid of Giza hosted a portal most considered particularly spectacular, as it opened up with a great hole in it.

The seven portals led to Rahir, or "New Terra" as it would later be known. Overall, it was much like the earth, but with a bit less gravity. The single moon's cycles, the length of days and years were roughly the same as Earth's, but the stars were different.

The native people appeared to be human and lived simple but carefree lives. They had boats that flew, were long-lived, and dwelt mostly in small villages outside of ancient ruins and beautiful gardens which dotted the landscape.

There were many more portals on Rahir, and it was through these portals that strange beings from other planets were observed coming and going, much as the Earthlings were. It was also said that in some of the portals on Rahir, you could not only travel back and forth through space, but through time as well! The luminorphs were much more plentiful on New Terra, as well.

To many Earthlings, this simple and safe interstellar travel seemed too good to be true. They still feared the events were some sort of prelude to an insidious extraterrestrial plot to undermine or invade our planet. Some religious fundamentalists thought it might be the work of the devil.

Inevitably, there were problems. Some people never returned from their journeys through the portals, which naturally caused grief among their families and friends left behind.

Soon, hundreds of people at the Stonehenge site had come and gone through the portal and some decided to move to New Terra permanently, bringing their belongings with them.

Sadly, at the other sites around the world, people were just beginning their exploration of the portals when war broke out. Despite contact with the luminorphs, the introduction of the trans-dimensional portals and the new enlightenment that they were offering to Old Earth, old conflicts remained heated and grew even hotter. The politically motivated and the ignorant could not adapt to the new mindset demanded by the appearance of the portals and their herald luminorphs, and did little to change their old ways. The events seemed to even increase mistrust and tension between peoples in some instances.

Then came reports of people who touched the larger translucent luminorphs and felt anxiety and dread instead of a mild euphoria and hope.

The war escalated. It was still not a major war as wars go, but missiles were launched, people died and then almost overnight, the luminorphs disappeared and the portals along with them, never to be seen again.

But that was then, and this is now.

That was Old Earth, at the last anyone knew of it.

This morning, one-hundred years later, the professor stood on this New Earth or New Terra, as the colonists insisted on calling it, which indeed has many trans-dimensional portals. In fact, thirty-six had been mapped across the planet (far more than recorded on any other planet) and even more remarkably, twenty-two of them are located here, in and around the small province of Validon.

The professor was an astronomer who worked at the local observatory. There were many observatories on New Terra, both ancient and modern, but his observatory was perhaps the largest. On the grounds of the observatory were many beautiful gardens on a large hill which was on the end of a peninsula jutting out into the Bay of Validon. It was surrounded by many other gardens and served as the main focal point in the province of Validon. It seemed like no matter where you went in Validon you could see the Observatory Gardens on the hill somewhere in the distance.

Across the river from the Observatory Gardens

was the capital city of Validon, New Cambridge, which had been shortened to simply Cambridge over the years. Many places had been named after towns and cities back on Old Earth by the people who colonized the planet - the hundreds who had dared to visit or decided to settle here and became stranded when the portals on Old Earth suddenly closed forever. On New Terra, one was able to enter many of these portals and travel to many different places throughout the cosmos, but unfortunately, the Old Earth was no longer one of them.

The largest university on the planet of New Terra was located in Cambridge. Our good professor had an important meeting at the university that morning but for the moment, was preoccupied.

The luminorph was aware of the professor's presence and indeed, seemed to go out of its way to approach him as he stood in his yard. The professor was particularly fascinated by the luminorphs. He studied them and followed them around, constantly making mental notes of their behaviour. Some folks might have assumed that he was a biologist, rather than an astronomer.

From experience he knew how to approach them without scaring them off. Slowly and carefully he reached out to touch it. It did not back away as they so often did and even seemed to nuzzle his outstretched hand like a purring kitten. One could not actually feel the body of this species of glowing, translucent luminorph (or "lumies" as people here sometimes liked to call them), but you could feel or rather, sense a sort of warmth to the touch. It felt especially soothing to the old man on this chilly Validon morning.

The luminorph lingered a while then moved on.

The professor watched it drift slowly out of sight as its light disappeared into the woods along the edge of the meadow.

The local train station had been built in the prevalent Victorian style of architecture in Validon. A few modern looking buildings and some rather ancient but well-kept looking structures could be spotted here and there, but the aesthetic preference of the colonists was clear.

Even the train which the professor boarded looked old-fashioned on the outside. The engine was circa nineteen-ought-something in appearance, complete with smoke stack and whistle. There was even a fancy red caboose. Yet inside it was clean and modern. The ride was smooth, quiet and fast. On board, people chatted softly with each other, read books and magazines or worked or entertained themselves on computers built into the seats.

The train was on its way to Cambridge as the Professor sat in silence, staring at the passing scenery outside the window as he always did. It was a short thirty minute trip to the capital city. It would have taken no time at all if the train did not make the frequent stops along the way to pick up other passengers.

On warmer days the professor would sometimes walk to work, which generally took about an hour. There was usually no hurry in this world. After all, this was New Terra, a small planet of many trans-dimensional portals where one could simply look at a map, locate the correct garden where one or several portals were located, go there and then casually stroll into a portal, which was usually set in an arch or gateway. You would then find yourself instantly transported to another part of New Terra, another planet, another galaxy, perhaps even another universe where time as we knew it, did not exist. On New Terra, space and time really were relative.

Not that the professor was a frequent explorer of the portals, even though he had a portal cluster near his garden.

A portal cluster was a phenomenon that consisted of two or more portals that appeared side by side next to one another. His cluster of three trans-dimensional portals were located in a folly on his property next to the yard. However, he entered the portals less and less over the years, and rarely explored any other portals located in Validon or beyond.

The folly was a stone structure built by his late father two decades earlier that was meant to look like an old ruin. It was on a hill next to the professor's house. A small stream found its way down from the foothills of tree-covered and well-worn mountains in the distance. The stream wound its way around the base of the hill then into the fields beyond.

The folly was modelled after a small castle ruin near Limerick, Ireland that was in a photo brought from Old Earth. One wall was built into a large outcrop of rocks along one side of the hill. This gave it a natural appearance from a distance.

The professor preferred ruins in which it was hard to tell at first glance if it was a man-made structure or natural rock formation. This psuedo-ruin now looked more like a genuine ruin than ever, for it had become overgrown with vines and small trees.

There were three stone arches in the courtyard below its main tower, and each was home to a trans-dimensional portals. This was not that unusual for New Terra. Most of the twenty-two portals that existed in Validon were located in follies or in people's gardens. They erected arches of stone or plant archways and gateways made of various shrubs and allowed vines to grow up around them.

Some folks who had the room liked to create stone grottoes around the portals, which were hidden among secret gardens within larger gardens.

Fortunately, there were no long lines of intergalactic tourists waiting to use the portals, for in such a large galaxy, the vast majority of the technologically advanced planets had no idea that New Terra existed, for they had no trans-dimensional portals of their own to take them to the world. But if you were one of the lucky few planets who did have these portals, you would find all thirty-six locations of the portals listed on the maps of New Terra.

It was common practice and considered neighbourly for anyone who had one or more trans-dimensional portals on their property to allow any wanderer, human or non-human who politely requests a visit, to enter any portal that they wished to explore, provided it was safe, of course.

It could be a risky or even dangerous undertaking to enter some portals, especially those that could transport you into other unexplored dimensions.

These extra-dimensional portals were timeless, so no matter how long one dwelt there, you would not age, but unfortunately, they were often unstable and could fluctuate or disappear unexpectedly.

These were banned from public use and labelled with a bright red 'X' on the maps, and those who had one of these portals would close them off or have a warning sign posted in front of it.

Tragically, people still went missing at times and no one could locate them. It was seldom talked about frankly among the populace but it was often assumed that these people had walked, either accidentally or intentionally, into an unstable portal.

Then there were the stories, like the one about the young man who had fallen in love with a woman he had met on one of his portal explorations. He went back through the portal, but could not find her. Unable to accept the idea that perhaps she did not want him, he believed that he had entered the wrong portal, especially since he was a frequent portal traveller. He assumed that he mixed up his portals and travelled endlessly from one to another, looking for her. In desperation, a lover whose mind has been clouded by unrequited love may enter an unstable portal through which there is often no return.

In fact, one could actually get mixed up and lost if one travelled to another world by portal and that world, in turn, has other portals which opened out into still other worlds with other portals and so on. Every portal opened to a different place. The same was true of portal clusters, whether there were two, four, seven, or the professor's three.

One of the professor's trans-dimensional portals opened out to the province of Pawzua in another part of New Terra. It was an exotic and beautiful tropical location near the equator. There were many small but mountainous islands and sandy beaches. There the natives steered lightweight fishing boats made of reeds and many thin but large gossamer-like sails which trapped the wind. New Terra, being somewhat smaller than our earth, had a bit less gravity, which combined with the local trade winds, could actually lift the boats off of the water and into the air, as long as there were but a handful of small boys on board or no more than two men per boat. They glided slowly just above the tree tops as they navigated their little boats along the many small streams and bays. It was quite a fantastic and yet oddly serene sight to behold.

The women and girls in the villages employed New Terra's lighter gravity, combined with the winds of Pawzua, to aid them in their gardening. There were many garden plots located on hillsides, leading down to the sea where they would pick fruit and vegetables, placing them in wide, shallow baskets suspended from large kites which remained aloft all day. There was a rope attached from their waists to the kite-suspended baskets, which would float above the ground next to them as they walked from plot to plot. When the day was done and the baskets had been emptied, they would have a bit of fun by climbing into the kite baskets and ride them through the air, suspended several feet off the ground over the hills, down to the sea.

The second portal took you to another world entirely. You would find yourself elsewhere in New Terra's solar system on the small icy moon known as Mimos, which orbited the beautiful ringed planet, Kala-Mai. There the portal opened out onto a scene of beautiful ice formations, crystalline ice caves and cliffs. Kala-Mai, the giant multi-colored ringed planet, much like our Saturn, engulfed half the sky and bathed the snow-covered landscape and mountains of ice in rainbow hues. Mimos had a breathable atmosphere but one had to remember to dress warmly before entering its portal.

The third portal opened into another dimension and was of course, risky to enter, since like other portals of the kind it could often be unstable and unpredictable. The professor had entered it only once, many years ago, and never attempted it again. It was shortly after his father died. His memory of the experience, like the experience itself, was like a dream from which he had been lucky to awaken.

He had been a somewhat younger and more foolish man back then, and blinded by grief. He did not really think it possible, but he was wishing that this strange portal to an unknown dimension could somehow lead him to the universe where the soul of his deceased father now dwelt.

Ignoring his late father's warning sign erected in front of the archway, he entered the portal to a world not drastically different from New Terra. It was green like Validon in the warmer months, but the terrain was flatter. There were no mountains in the distance and very few hills. Long grasses and sprawling pasture land greeted him instead. There was an old barn in front of him. Behind him he heard a voice call out. He turned around and realized that he was standing on wooden steps leading up to the front porch of a farm house. A young girl came out of the screen door in the front of the house, onto the porch. She walked towards him smiling and said something to him. The individual words sounded like English but the way she strung them together did not make sense to him. When he could not adequately reply, she frowned and went back in.

He thought he heard another sound coming

from the barn which should have been behind him, but when he turned to look in that direction the landscape had drastically changed.

Suddenly it was no longer day but had turned to night and he found himself in a cool, gray desert. There were surreal rock formations and oddly shaped bare trees. There was a starless glowing pale gray sky above. Then he noticed another portal. It was huge. It must have been fifty meters high and thirty meters wide, jet black against the starless light gray sky. Suddenly, strange little shapes flew out of the giant black rectangular shape. They looked a bit like luminorphs at first but darted to and fro much faster, making strange and eerie little sounds like crows but higher pitched. They almost sounded like children crying. They were colorful, in stark contrast to the gray landscape around him. Their shapes were amorphous but angular.

Then the professor noticed that there was a spark of colour in the middle of the great black rectangle in front of him. The spark grew in size and quickly became large patterns of multi-coloured geometric shapes not unlike the ones that you experience when you close and rub your eyes. It grew larger still and began to engulf him.

He became frightened. He wanted to run away but where to? He turned in the opposite direction, took two steps and found himself back home on the opposite side of the stone archway in the folly back on New Terra. With great relief, he realized that he was safe and sound.

Now it was years later and as the professor sat on board the train he had other things on his mind as he looked out the window, watching the

Observatory Gardens come closer into view.

The observatory had been built by the first pilgrims from Old Earth about eighty years ago on the site of a crumbling ancient observatory, which in turn had been built by the indigenous people. The gardens were mostly English style but also French, Italian and Japanese in design as they fanned out in all directions, covering the hill and beyond for many acres.

Numerous streams, canals, low stone walls and hedgerows crisscrossed the landscape, punctuated with the occasional ruin: follies built by the Old Earth settlers as well as genuine ruins, built by the native population before the luminorphs first arrived on this world. For even here, the luminorphs were not native to this planet but had arrived many generations ago.

However, unlike Old Earth, there had always been portals on the planet. The ancestors of the native population had built stone arches around them and worshiped them as gifts from the gods that were only meant to be used by the 'chosen ones'. So by law and custom, only the Elders of the various tribes, along with a select few, were allowed to enter the portals. Any extra-terrestrials that emerged from the other side of the portals, especially if they were non-human, were often either worshiped or feared, depending on their appearance. This had frequently lead to conflict.

Then the luminorphs arrived and with them even more portals opened up. Everyone in all the tribes of New Terra then began to enter them. Eventually, when all people could make contact with other worlds, ignorance and superstition gave way to knowledge and enlightenment.

Then, one-hundred years ago, even more portals opened up as the first people from the planet earth, including the professor's grandparents, arrived.

A voice suddenly said, "Next stop, Validon Observatory. New Cambridge, five minutes."

The professor paid little attention as he continued staring out of the window of his train compartment, still lost in thought about the history and splendor of New Terra, brought about by his encounter with the small luminorph earlier that morning.

The professor's reverie was interrupted by the sensation of a tiny head peering over his shoulder. It was connected to a long, snake-like neck. All the old man could see at that moment was the back of a tiny head in place of the window he was trying to look through. Then the tiny head at the end of the extremely long neck turned around, revealing a tiny face which looked into the professor's eyes and said, "How's the view?"

"It was better before", said the professor, chuckling.

The tiny head and impossibly long neck belonged to one of his colleagues, Dr. Frav Raal. He was from another planet, which the professor had never managed to pronounce properly. Dr. Raal had a brilliant mind but somewhat impish sense of humour.

"Aren't you getting off at the observatory, Ian?" asked Dr. Raal.

"No", said the professor, "special meeting at the university this morning, Frav. Aren't you going?"

"Indeed I am", said Dr. Raal. "I didn't know that you were invited, too."

"Indeed I was", said the professor.

However, levity was short-lived these days. It had been made public several weeks ago that a signal from deep space had been intercepted. There was a rumour of war elsewhere in the galaxy. There had been no wars on any known planets since the one on Old Earth, one-hundred years ago. War was thought to have been extinct. This was disturbing. Many people had become uneasy with this news and were even becoming a little distrustful of any extra-terrestrial visitors newly arrived to the planet.

Yet wiser men, like the professor, his colleagues at the observatory, the university and elsewhere, did not, in fact, take this "threat," as some were beginning to call it, all that seriously. Not yet, anyway. It was disturbing, yes, but no need for alarm. Nevertheless, this sort of attitude tended to cause consternation in others who were growing increasingly anxious.

The special meeting that the professor and the others were attending had been called to discuss this very situation. Besides the professor's colleagues (fellow astronomers and university staff), there were two government officials present, along with a reporter. One of the government officials acted as the chairman of the meeting.

The meeting was largely unproductive. No hard facts had been discussed and there was no new information. The professor's presence at the meeting had been largely ignored so he wondered what he was doing there. A higher ranking government official failed to show up, so the meeting was adjourned early.

"Just as well", the professor thought.

Then just as they were leaving, the chairman received a message.

"All right", he said, "emergency meeting tomorrow morning, seven a.m., sharp."

Everyone except the professor let out a loud groan. He would have, too, had he been paying attention.

Late that night the professor was awakened by his barking dog again. He sighed and grumbled to himself saying, "he plays with that cat all day long then barks at him when he's outside the window. Why does he do that?"

However, when the professor came to the window, it was no cat that his dog was barking at this time.

The professor gasped. There, just outside his window stood a brightly glowing luminorph, the height of a tall man. The professor was actually a bit frightened as well as fascinated. He put on his heavy coat and crept outside into the darkness and the snow.

The luminorph was one of the Old Ones as the natives referred to them, also known as zephyr spirits. They normally dwelt in more remote areas, gliding and dancing on the wind in the lands of the ancients. They were the largest and most mysterious of the luminorphs, and had large and colourful translucent glowing forms that undulated and shimmered in the gentle breezes of spring and summer. They were rarely seen and rarely came to earth and yet astonishingly, here was one, standing in his yard. And in winter.

After a while, the professor was finally able to swallow. He slowly reached out his hand. It had been a long time since he had touched one of the larger luminorphs. He felt the mild shock and with it, a peculiar sensation.

It was an odd mix of dread that gave way to a glimmer of hope. There was a voice of sorts inside his brain that seemed to be telling him something.

Was it true that the Old Ones could actually communicate telepathically? It was more of a feeling than any form of words: there was something important that was happening tomorrow and his presence was required.

Suddenly, a gust of chill wind sent the luminorph skyward, temporarily blocking out the stars as it glided up and over the hill and pseudo-ruins next door.

It was like it had all been a dream.

At dawn, his little barking dog woke the professor once again. He raced to the front window, wondering if the luminorph had returned. This time it turned out to be the dark figure of a person in a wide-brimmed fedora hat and trench coat standing on his front stoop. His early twentieth century-style door bell chimed.

The professor put on his old coat and greeted the person at the door. It was Dr. Ivy Takai-Rothstein, the president of the science and astronomy department at Cambridge University. She was the liaison between the university and the observatory and had attended the meeting the day before.

"You didn't forget our emergency meeting this morning did you, Ian?", she said.

"Uh...no. No, of course not", the professor lied. Or rather, it was not a lie, since he had not paid any attention in the first place.

He did want to lie, though. He wanted to tell the woman that he was not feeling well. He wanted to tell her that he was an old man who needed his sleep and besides, no one even seemed to notice that he was there yesterday, anyway.

Then he remembered his dreamlike encounter with the Old One last night. He was not sure if it was telepathy or his own subconscious, but he had a feeling that he really should attend, after all.

He invited his fellow professor in while he got ready. As they left his house the professor looked at her fedora and trench coat and remarked, "Ivy, you look like a female Humphrey Bogart in that outfit."

"Who?" she asked.

"Never mind", the professor sighed.

The news spread quickly throughout New Terra. Within minutes, everyone knew.

According to reports, the signal that had been intercepted earlier, though weak and only partially understood, was definitely a transmission being sent by a planet under siege by an invading force from another planet.

People were becoming frightened. Worse still, what if this invading force did not stop there? What if they kept on, spreading throughout the galaxy and arrived on New Terra? If they discovered the portals they would have easy access to many other worlds as well. They could conceivably take over the entire universe!

The chairman shouted, "Order!"

This time, there were more government officials and reporters, along with several space technicians there.

There were those at the meeting who were clearly agitated and were beginning to take their fear and frustration out on any extra-terrestrials that were present. The professor's associate, Dr. Raal and several other beings from other planets did not seem concerned enough with this dire situation to suit the aggressors. "Why don't those of you from the more technologically advanced planets help us?" they asked.

"You have spaceships, don't you? Can't you amass a great fleet of ships equipped with powerful weapons to intercept them before they get here?"

The professor could not help but notice that the eyes of some of his fellow humans lit up, revealing a tinge of exhilaration along with their fear.

At this point, the professor spoke up, "You're jumping to conclusions. In the first place, do we really know how reliable this information is? In the second place, do we even know if this so-called invading force is headed this way or if they can even travel this distance?"

The chairman replied, "for your information, Professor Pearson, though we don't know from where the signal originated, we do know that it was received at a point in deep space less than one quarter light year from here - well within range of many of today's more advanced star-ships. Also, it was clearly intended for us since it was transmitted in English. It is obviously meant to-" the chairman was interrupted by one of the technicians who began whispering something in his ear.

In the meantime, the professor thought to himself, "English? The transmission is in English? Hmm... I suppose it's possible. English-speaking people from New Terra have settled on other planets by way of the portals."

Then the chairman spoke in a loud voice, "I have been informed that we now have a more complete computer-enhanced recording of the message. I regret to inform you that it sounds quite ominous. We will play it for you now."

Everyone instantly went silent. The transmission popped and crackled. Between bouts of loud static you could here snippets of fearful male voices saying things like, "We interrupt this program...difficulty with our transmission...enemy tripod machines...vanguard of an invading army...heat ray...enemy now turns east crossing Passaic River into... we believe alien invasion from..."

Strange thought it was, the message sounded oddly familiar to the professor.

The transmission continued: "... they landed at Grover's Mill, New Jersey..."

Then the professor remembered. It all came back to him now. "Grover's Mill. Of course", he muttered to himself.

Then he began to laugh quite raucously.

People stared at him assuming he had gone mad with fear.

Of course, it was not fear but relief and great amusement. He had not laughed so hard in years. Being a student of late nineteenth as well as twentieth century history, the professor recalled learning of an incident involving two of his favorite figures from that period: H.G. Wells and Orson Welles.

Yes, this was it. This was that infamous radio program based on "The War of the Worlds", that caused such a panic among those twentieth century rubes and now, almost two-hundred years later, it was happening again.

Amazingly, the signal from that broadcast had travelled through space all this time, only to wind up here.

As the professor regained his composure, he explained to everyone, with glee tinged with cynicism, what had just happened.

He noted that even though they lived in a world where they had things like trans-dimensional portals, which granted them access to many other worlds, they still remained gullible, wide-eyed, innocent rubes down deep and proceeded to tactlessly tell everyone so.

Afterwards, the professor paused and gazed around the room at the embarrassed faces. Then he sighed and smiled kindly at them while saying in a softer voice, "oh well, maybe after all is said and done, it's not so bad to still be a wide-eyed innocent."

Then the professor politely excused himself, explaining that he needed to spend more time at his observatory. As he was leaving the room he could hear Dr. Raal chuckling in his peculiar extra-terrestrial sort of way, while Dr. Takai-Rothsein said meekly, "Thank you, Professor."

He said, "You're welcome," without looking back.

The professor walked across the bridge leading to the Observatory Gardens.

It had been a gray morning but now the sun was peaking through the clouds. The light illuminated the icicles hanging from the wrought iron lamp posts, as well as the trees and topiaries that were waiting for him on the other side.

The professor had a special fondness for

topiaries, with their eccentric and whimsical shapes, now half-covered in snow. They were quite prevalent in the Observatory Gardens as well as all the surrounding gardens of Validon.

He walked among the numerous box yews of many shapes and sizes, the small foot bridges, archways of stone and hedge, gates, scattered ruins, numerous streams and canals, beautiful fountains of all kinds, all fanning out in many directions as far as the eye could see.

The professor walked up the hill and entered the observatory. A short time later he emerged out onto one of the observatory's brick terraces and quietly looked down onto the sprawling landscape below him. To him this was more beautiful than any of the stars, galaxies or giant multi-colored nebulae that he gazed at through the observatory's giant telescope.

In a quiet way, this place was even more wondrous to him than any exotic planet that he had ever visited in the trans-dimensional portals, as well.

Indeed, he was like Mole. The professor held a withering copy of *The Wind in the Willows* in his hand. His grandmother had brought it from Old Earth, and had given it to him when he was a child.

He read, "...the Mole saw clearly that he was an animal of tilled field and hedge-row, linked to the plowed furrow, the frequented pasture, the lane of evening lingerings, the cultivated garden-plot. For others the asperities, the stubborn endurance, or the clash of actual conflict, that went with nature in the rough; he must be wise, must keep to the pleasant places in which his lines were laid and which held adventure enough, in their way, to last for a lifetime."

Then he looked at the scenery a little while longer before going back inside.

The Life of a Romantic

By Nanna P. Vej

In a world where rocks are generally considered to have psychic abilities, the people of the crowded streets of the city Terry did not find it strange at all that a young man should bend down to a small rock at the side of the road. "How is that meeting gonna go?" he asked in a loud voice akin to what one might use when addressing small children.

The rock began to vibrate.

"Is it gonna be a good meeting?" he continued, and the rock was now enthusiastically jumping around like a dog wagging its tale. Despite presumably having such wonderful abilities, the rocks had never learned to speak, and so their message was forever trapped in their core. Young Steve knew this and gave up with a sigh. Ahead of him lay the tall grim building in which he worked, and within it a table full of corporate types ready to slay him.

His only friend in the company, Harriet, greeted him as he walked through his usual floor toward the conference room; it seemed as though the temperature had gone below zero degrees.

He did all he could, but he knew that it just was not good enough as people started to gather their things to leave after his poor performance. His boss, Mr. Boston, walked up to him after the meeting with a warm smile on his face. Steve did not trust it one bit.

"Steve!" He exclaimed and put an arm around his shoulder. "That went quite well didn't it?"

"I don't know about that, sir-" Steve began, but was interrupted.

"There is just one thing," Mr. Boston said and let his smile fade. "Times are changing, Steve," he continued and began to walk, forcing Steve to follow, "and the company simply can't afford...."

Steve stopped listening. He knew it had been coming, and yet for some reason he was not sad, he just felt empty.

"...I wish you all the luck in the world," Mr. Boston finished after a long speech, shook his hand and walked away, thereby leaving Steve behind forever.

He slowly walked to his desk and started packing his things into the same box he had once used to bring them into the firm. Harriet tried to strike up a positive conversation, but he just could not fake it, and she soon gave up. She did, however, give him a long hug and said 'goodbye' as he left. Despite their warm goodbye, Steve knew that she, too, had left him behind, already part of her past. He was starting to feel as if that was where he belonged in general, in the past. He felt as a ghost and haunted the road to his car. Without thinking, without feeling, he set the box inside and began to drive home to his small apartment at the other end of town.

Emptiness. Everything seemed to be covered in it, filled with it and held together by it. Everything but Sarah, she was not empty. She was more like a rock in stormy weather. Although, instead of being his shelter against the wind, she was the rock the wind flung him into. She would most likely come around that evening; at least earlier she had talked about doing so.

His thoughts were interrupted by a siren just behind him. He glanced into the rearview mirror and saw that he had a police car on his tail, his next glance went to the speedometer. "Fuck!" He reduced his speed and was about to pull over when his eyes quickly flicked to the mirror again, to confirm the police officer was indeed after him and not some other fellow. For a split second he saw a young girl in the backseat smiling at him, then she was gone. He jerked his head around in shock, but the backseat was sure enough empty.

He arrived home half an hour later, with a five hundred dollar fine. Empty, he was empty.

"Where have you been?" asked Sarah, who was waiting outside the apartment building. He looked at his watch in bewilderment, it was way past six. How could it have gotten that late? He had left the office several hours earlier than usual.

"Work ran late," he lied.

She sent him skeptic look, but then she smiled and kissed him. "How was your day then?" she asked as they walked up the stairs to the eleventh floor together. He would have taken the elevator, but Sarah always insisted on taking the stairs; it was a nightmare.

He had other things to worry about this time, though. How was he to tell her? Tell her that not only had he gotten a bloody speeding ticket, but he had also lost his job and had a strange hallucination? He was not actually planning on mentioning the last one... possibly not the first one either. He should probably just tell her he was out of a job, but how could he possibly tell her that?

"It was pretty good," he said and sent a small smile to assure her of his fake sincerity. *She is beautiful*, he thought to himself. Her curly hair partly hidden under a winter beanie, her neck covered in a blue, green and grey scarf that was way too long. She seemed so calm, as she always did. Like a rock in a storm.

They finally arrived on the eleventh floor where he unlocked his door and allowed her to walk inside ahead of him. "You look tired, how about I cook tonight?" she suggested. He merely smiled back in exhaustion, and she got the hint.

He loved it when she cooked, especially when she herself suggested it so he did not have to feel bad. His cooking was horrible, and he always felt a bit embarrassed when he was the one to cook for her. So while she went through his kitchen looking for something edible, he went through the mail, trying to shake off the emptiness. There was nothing of interest. There never really was.

"Steve," a voice said behind him. He whirled around and in horror saw the young girl he had thought he had seen in the car. She was leaning against the wall, dressed in a long black coat with her hands in her pockets. "Steve," she said again and looked thoughtful, as if she tasted the name. "A friend and I always use to make up humorous scenarios about people or things named 'Steve'," she said, more to the air than to him. He wanted to ask her how the hell she had gotten in, but part of him knew that she had not entered at all.

"What are you staring at?" Sarah asked in amusement from the kitchen door. He looked at her and tried to smile while he shrugged his shoulders to excuse his strange behavior. He succeeded in looking calm when really he felt terrified. He had a bad feeling — or perhaps it was a good one — that when he turned his head around again the young woman would be gone.

She was.

He really was freaked out, but a sensible voice deep inside told him it was merely a reaction to the stress after a horrid day, and he should not take notice. A voice even deeper inside tried to tell him that something was dreadfully wrong, but he decided to ignore it, for now.

They had a fairly pleasant, if simple, dinner, after which they lay on the couch in silence. It often struck Steve that the woman in his arms was beyond amazing, but that in her world there was only satisfaction. She may be happy with him, but he felt she would be equally as happy without him.

"I really care about you, you know?" he said and gave her a kiss. She hugged him closer before she answered with, "I'd totally forgotten, but you had a meeting today right? How did that go?"

Steve sighed. It was not that she brought up the dreadful meeting that bothered him, it was her inability to realize how it hurt him to never hear anything sweet or kind from her, other than what her kisses would tell him.

"It went fine," he mumbled. He was aware of the fact that she did not even realize that he was expecting her to say something, anything back. In her world her response was perfectly normal.

When Sarah left Steve allowed himself to plop into a huge chair and bury his face in his hands. He still was not sad, still just empty.

"It's because she's a cynic, you know," a voice said, and terror struck him again. There she was again, sitting on the couch, with her feet casually planted on the table. She smiled at him, as if to calm him down.

It did not calm him down.

She seemed to understand and extended a hand. "Danielle," she introduced herself.

He was not quite sure why, but he could not think of anything else to do but to accept her hand and offer, "Steve."

"Yeah, I've heard."

Steve then decided that he had made enough conversation with his newfound sense of insanity for that evening and grabbed a book, which he tried to read. Every time he looked out of the corner of his eye, however, she was still there, smiling, patiently waiting for him to give in. He did not manage to read a single line. Finally he put down the book and looked back at her.

"Calm down, chap," she said and leaned further back on the couch. "It's not like you're mad."

He raised an eyebrow.

"Well, actually," she added more to herself than to him, "I don't know if that's quite true."

"You can't be true, so I must be insane," he said and frantically looked through his pockets for a smoke.

"Well, if you *know* that I cannot be real, then surely that should speak against you being insane," she answered cheerfully.

"My reason tells me that you cannot be real," he said while trying to light the cigarette with shaking hands. "But other than that, you could have fooled me."

"Maybe I'm not unreal," she leaned in over the table, still with a huge smile on her lips.

He thought the thought through for a little while. He still felt completely determined that she had to be his imagination, but it sure was a nice thought to think that perhaps she was not. He had never been one to believe in anything extraordinary, but he had always wanted to, and if he was going to go mad he may as well take the opportunity to believe something.

"So what are you, then?" He asked, hoping that the answer would be accompanied with some divine evidence. "An angel? A ghost?"

"Well, no, not really," she replied after a little while. "Well, actually, I might be."

Ashes dropped onto his shoe and he noticed that he had not been paying his cigarette any attention at all.

"Let's just agree that I *am,*" she concluded. "Then, again," she began, thoughtfully, "that might not even be the case."

It struck him that she knew just as little as he did, at least when it came to her own existence. Then he remembered what she had said when she had first appeared on his couch.

"What did you mean earlier?" he asked, "when you said Sarah is a cynic?"

"Sarah?" she asked and seemed to slip back into her own thoughts. "Is that her name? I had a roommate sort of thing named Sarah once."

Then she seemed to return to the real world again, if such a thing could be possible, and said, "Well, she is. A cynic, I mean."

"She doesn't seem very cynical to me," Steve countered, testing the waters of this conversation with the maybe ghost/angel/hallucination.

"Forget your everyday definition of a cynic, and take this instead: There are three kinds of people, right?" She sat up and started to do frantic hand gestures, and he could tell that whatever he was about to hear was her life philosophy. "There are the romantics, the ones who despite the cruelty of the world still believe in happiness and miracles, even if they claim otherwise. They will never be satisfied, for they are always looking for something impossible. Then there are the cynics, the ones who have realized the ways of the world and accepted it as is, the ones who won't look for love, but merely for a comfortable, happy position until it is no longer satisfactory, as they know nothing lasts forever. The worst of the lot are the almost cynics, who are really romantics desperately trying to swap sides. Some succeed, though most don't. They know the way of the world, they logically know, but they do not *feel* it, and so still hope that things will turn out differently for them. Which actually means that they are still romantics, hoping that turning to reason will stop them from getting hurt. They will do whatever it takes to make the world aware of their reasonable views, while quietly thinking that things could surely be different."

"And Sarah's a cynic?" he asked, and although he did not really want to admit it, he saw the reasoning in her point of view and recognized Sarah from her definition.

"She is, and I can tell that you agree." Danielle's smile faded a bit, though she still looked happy. Happy and content, and somehow he knew that her lecture was done for the day.

"Can you just look over there?" she asked and pointed at the wall behind her.

Steve did not move. "Why?"

"It's just more dramatic that way, you know?"

He indulged her, and, as expected, she was gone when he turned around again.

Steve did not have much luck sleeping that

night, but with all the strange and terrible things the day had brought him, his head was too full to make him sad. Instead he felt fed up… and yet empty.

The next day he spent bent over newspaper and searching the internet to find his next pit stop in life. In other words, he was job hunting. While hyped up on more coffee than he had ever contained, his head was puzzling with new possibilities, each more unlikely than the last. Though the more he tried to focus on finding a new and realistic job, his mind slipped off to Danielle's words. He found himself agreeing more and more. Sarah was a cynic and he could not stand it. Could not stand her peace, could not stand how she was always perfectly fine with things that bothered him immensely.

Around two o'clock he decided to take a break and do a bit of grocery shopping. He walked straight to the dairy section with some strange idea about living on yogurt and cornflakes, though as soon as he saw the cooler he hesitated. A young woman in a long black coat was standing with her back to him, staring at the milk, cream, yogurt and various other dairy products. For a second he wondered if perhaps she was a girl living in the area, whom he might have seen before. With the stress that took over him the night before, surely he could have projected the image of someone he already had in his head, subconsciously of course.

Then an old lady walked straight toward her as if she did not see the young girl at all, and though Danielle jumped aside, he was still pretty sure that he was the only one who could see her. Obviously he could not avoid her if she meant to ambush him in the dairy aisle, so he decided to walk up to her.

"Bloody rude," Danielle accused the old lady as he approached. It was like she knew he had been watching her, which she most likely did.

"Yeah," he answered, doubting if he really meant it; the old lady could not help it after all.

"So, have you given our conversation from last night some thought?"

He was not comfortable responding at all, since people around him would surely notice if he starting having a conversation with the air in the middle of a grocery store. Feeling a bit nuts was one thing, having people notice was an entirely different thing. So, instead he just looked around.

She understood and nodded. "Let's go somewhere else."

He tried to ignore her while he did the rest of his shopping, which was fairly hard to do, seeing as she kept talking, talking of everything and nothing. He sort of wanted to find her annoying, but at times he could not help but smile at her random and surely crazy comments. Somehow she was not really a creepy insane segment in his head, more like a cheerful little sister you try to ignore, despite wanting to laugh.

"Oh, look!" Danielle exclaimed while he was picking out some detergent. He looked where she pointed and saw a young man who had jogged into the store, trying to maintain a jog while doing his shopping. Steve had seen him before but he had never seen the amusing point before Danielle brought it to his attention. "That dude is legendary, he just keeps going, how epic is that?" she asked and laughed. He could tell she was not mocking the fellow, but truly admired him.

When he finished shopping she led him to a

park in the middle of Terry.

"You know, I've never understood the name of this city," she commented.

"I've never really thought of it," Steve answered. "I grew up here."

"I never knew anyone named Terry, I did, however, dream of working with Terry Rossio and Ted Elliot. I also quite liked Terry Pratchett's writing, even though I never read that much."

"What did you dream of working with?" he asked, having completely forgotten that he did not think she was real.

"I wanted to be a writer for a while, before I realized everyone wanted to be a writer, and everyone wrote better than me." She laughed, she always seemed to laugh.

They settled under a huge tree, half buried in snow. At first he hesitated about sitting on the ground, but she merely sat down, so in the end he did so as well, ignoring the wet and cold feeling.

"I always just wanted to be an architect," he said and sighed, "and I was, for a while."

"You're still an architect, just an architect without a job," Danielle countered.

"Fucking Mr. Boston," he mumbled under his breath.

"My geography teacher was named Mr. Boston," she commented.

"How can you possibly have had a life? What are you?" Steve demanded, still bewildered, although at ease with her dubious existence.

"I thought we finished this conversation already?" Danielle squinted at him, like she was sure they had, but then again, maybe was just trying to convince him they had.

"But your comments make no sense at all," he argued, and raising his hands to indicate their conversation added, "*This* makes no sense at all."

"So your girlfriend is a cynic, eh?" Danielle tried to change the subject.

"Yeah, I suppose she is," Steve gave in.

"You hate it."

"I don't hate her, I care for her very much," he rebuffed.

"That's not what I said, I said you hate *it*," Danielle clarified.

"Perhaps so," Steve admitted.

"Definitely so," Danielle pushed. For some reason she still smiled.

"How can you have had a life?" Steve asked again, to turn the conversation over on her.

"Do you really wanna know?" Danielle squinted at him again, as if she was not convinced he really wanted to have this conversation.

"Yeah, I wanna know why the hell this has happened." He truly was ready to listen.

"Well, I was a duck," Danielle began, and Steve dropped back knowing he would not hear a word of sense. "A duck among ducks," she laughed proudly. "I was a funky duck though, the most funky duck. I was so full of funk and the other ducks were like, 'You're *the* duck!' and then I was like, 'Nah, you guys are *the* ducks!'" She cracked up and he, too, had to crack a small smile, even though he really just wanted to shout *wtf*.

"And then," she tried to breathe so she could continue. "I was turned into a human, forever doomed to be clumsy and inelegant in every way, because really I'm just a duck in a human form. But please believe me; once upon a time I was funky!"

She laughed again.

"That didn't even come close to explaining anything," he sighed.

"Did it have to?"

"Very philosophical, Yoda." He looked out over the field, watching the few people who were out and about on a Tuesday afternoon. Then he caught a glimpse of Harriet who was making a snowman with her husband and children.

"You know her?" Danielle asked when she noticed his attention had found another target.

"I work with her. Well, used to," he corrected himself. "Her name is Harriet."

"Harriet," Danielle thought aloud. "A friend of mine once dated a girl named Harriet."

"Why do you keep doing that?" Steve asked.

"Doing what?"

"Commenting on names."

She shrugged her shoulders before she caught sight of two young girls. "You know that movie *Back to the Future*?"

"Yes?" he asked in puzzlement.

"Well, look at those two girls, I bet you they are your daughters from the future."

She truly was random, he thought.

"And they are here to break you and Sarah up, so that you can be with Harriet who is their mother. You are fucking up the timeline, mate!" Danielle joked and laughed.

Steve turned toward a rock lying next to him half covered in snow. "Is she insane?" he asked, and predictably it started vibrating, though not as enthusiastically as the pebble from the day before.

Danielle continued to giggle. "Do you ever get anything out of that?" she asked.

"No, not really," Steve sighed before asking, "Why are you here Danielle?"

"Ah!" she exclaimed, her smile fading, "finally you ask the right question. I am here because you are a romantic Steve, a romantic in a gray world, a romantic who has broken the rules."

"What rules?" Steve asked in bewilderment.

"You fell in love with a cynic," Danielle answered and promptly disappeared.

"Oh, for fuck's sake!" Steve exclaimed and stood up. "Danielle!" he called out. He stopped himself before he called out again; people were beginning to stare, including Harriet.

With Danielle's illogical words on his mind, he called Sarah that night. She seemed busy, but still he did not let her go, he wanted to hear her voice. She always sounded like she was ignoring him when they talked on the phone. He knew she did not mean to, but it really got to him anyway.

"I should probably go again," he finally mumbled when he could not stand it anymore.

"See you sometime next week, eh babe?" Sarah asked. Somehow he felt that they could see each other once every six months and it would make no difference to her. Not that he thought that she was about to leave him for someone else or anything, she cared for him, though not enough to say anything of the kind.

The next couple of days he heard not a word from Sarah nor Danielle. Not until Saturday morning, when he woke up staring into the young blue eyes belonging to Danielle.

"Morning, Mister!" She exclaimed after he had gotten over the shock.

"What the hell, Danielle!" Steve clutched the blanket close to him, embarrassed to have a young girl in his bedroom while he slept, even if she might not exist.

"Get up, Mr. Steve, 'cause we've got a mission ahead of us," Danielle declared with some very sincerely fake seriousness.

It was still dark outside; then again it was always dark outside this time of year. "Can't I imagine this a bit later?" he asked and fell back in bed.

"Of course you can't, silly, come on!" She left, probably so he could get dressed before she dragged him to the elevator.

"Where are we going?"

"To get coffee."

"Hmm," he considered, "that doesn't sound like a bad idea at all. Though it would have been a lot more efficient if you would just have let me sleep."

"Have you not missed me at all?" she jokingly asked.

"Well, I do have some questions," just as he said it the elevator door opened at the seventh floor, where an old gentleman was waiting. He sent Steve a suspicious look, but then he took the chance and joined him in the lift.

"You're scaring the poor old fella," Danielle mock-whispered, grinning, "talking to yourself and all."

He sent her an annoyed look, which she merely returned with a giggle. They went to a coffee shop around the corner where he unsurely ordered a single cup of coffee. "Rude bastard," Danielle commented in an offended way, but at seeing his suddenly sad face, she broke into a grin. "Come on!" she prodded and he followed her with his coffee to go. Magically when they went outside she, too, had a cup of steaming hot coffee.

"So why is it breaking the rules, me dating a cynic?" Steve asked while walking down the still deserted street, bathed in the first streaks of morning sun.

"Oh, but you know, Steve," Danielle answered, "it's not a good idea. Though now the damage is done, you love her and so that is that."

"I don't-" he began but she interrupted him.

"Let me finish, mate. I was in your situation once, I'm a romantic, too, you know, though I tried to join the almost Cynics, because I was going out with a pure cynic. I could tell he cared and all but I seriously hated being the one who cared the most, you know?"

"How can you even have had a life?" Steve asked again.

"Dude!" Danielle exclaimed, "you ain't fucking listening."

"I am, though," he said, "I know what you are saying, and you are quite right, but I just can't let her go."

"It's her you want, eh?" She was squinting at him again.

"Yeah." The word was heavy, hard to say.

"Well, matey, that's what I'm here for."

"How does that even make any sense?"

"You ask too many damn questions," Danielle observed and smiled again.

"Why are you so happy?"

She sighed and shook her head without letting the smile go. "Dear Steve, there is a lesson to be learned."

"Where are we going, anyway?" he asked and

looked around.

Danielle merely pointed and he followed her hand with his eyes. She was pointing at a grand building, which he knew to be an honored old architectural firm. It lay miles away from his apartment, though, and he could not make sense of how they had made it there so easily, and fast. Time just seemed to bend when Danielle was around.

He looked at her like a huge human question mark and she merely pointed at the building again as the only explanation. They crossed the road to get closer before he saw a small note outside the building that said they were looking for a fully educated and experienced architect.

"I don't get it," Steve said in bewilderment, "no proper firm looks for architects by a note on the wall."

She pointed at the wall again. The note was gone.

"What is up with this?" Steve asked loudly, half amazed, half annoyed. People started to look at him. "That is happening increasingly these days," he mumbled once people had forgotten the lunatic arguing with the wall and gone about their business.

"Well, this firm really is looking for people, they just don't know it yet," Danielle explained.

"What does that mean?"

"It means it will take you to make them realize," Danielle proclaimed proudly.

"That's fucking rubbish." Steve stared her in the eyes.

"You're fucking rubbish!" she exclaimed.

"Your mum is fucking rubbish!" he yelled back, and once again people turned to stare. Danielle and Steve stared back at them, though they only saw

Steve staring at them, all alone. Then they both cracked up.

"Someday, you will be a great architect, and Mr. Boston will be living in a box opposite a hobo, who shall ignore him every time he waves at him in his loneliness," Danielle confided with a sly smile on her lips.

"Is that a promise?" Steve did not really want to admit he kind of liked the sound of that prediction.

"No, not even close, but still, it's a dream. A dream worth fighting for."

"Hmm."

After having fought his way home in the freezing cold, Steve spent his day in front of the computer, considering writing an email to the company Danielle had taken him to. Several times he began and then deleted what he had written. He was sure, why did he not do it? It seemed a perfectly reasonable thing to do; it was just that the whole Danielle thing was still really strange.

His thoughts were interrupted by the doorbell. When he opened the door Sarah almost fell into his arms, she was not crying, but he knew that had she been any other woman she probably would have. For a split second he thought he saw Danielle in the hallway, she winked at him. He closed the door and took Sarah into the living room. It was nothing too horrid, just a bad day at work, and though he felt sorry for her, he could not help but be happy that she had come to him.

The whole evening they lay in each others' arms, talking of everything and nothing. It was a rare happening, but it was wonderful when it did happen, and this was probably the most successful example. She really made him smile and laugh, their humor was the same. Their way of thinking was in many ways the same, except words that did not even seem part of her vocabulary were burning their way through his head. He was holding on to his rock in the middle of a horrible storm and for once he felt that the rock was holding on to him as well. He somehow did not mind that she did not say anything at all of what was going on inside, because he understood, she was a cynic, it just was not her way. He understood.

He stroked her hair and allowed himself to fall asleep fully dressed in her arms.

The next morning they had breakfast together in a silence that was far from awkward before she headed off to work and he lied about working from home that day. He later convinced himself that it was not lying at all, seeing as he spent the day drawing the designs for a building that would never be.

"Write that damn email," Danielle's voice demanded from the shadows sometime around lunch.

"I will," he said without looking up. Her presence no longer surprised him. He was starting to think that she was some kind of escaped part of him that was trying to get his attention.

"Then why the hell have you hesitated?"

"Haven't a clue, but no worry, I will," he said while still drawing, "though I think I might write a letter instead."

"Classy," she commented and settled in on his couch. They sat in silence for the next few minutes until she finally said, "Well, I should let you work then."

"Okay, see you later, Danielle," he mumbled, still very distracted by his drawing.

She smiled and then disappeared. He did not realize, but he had grown accustomed to her presence and he knew he would see her again very soon.

The next day Steve was ready with his masterpiece and he felt like showing it to the whole world. So he sat down and scribbled a job application and went to mail it along with his drawing.

He was not quite sure why, but he decided to sit down on a small staircase outside a private house not far from the mailbox. It was as if he was waiting for something, but whether it was the mailman or perhaps for Danielle to show, he could not say. Maybe it was both. He lit a cigarette while waiting, trying to curl up closer to himself, to find shelter from the cold.

Sure enough Danielle did appear as she always did, suddenly sitting next to him. She was smoking too, just not a cigarette.

"Why are you smoking a pipe?" Steve asked in amusement and ignored the lady passing by who sent him a disturbed look.

"I bought it with a friend a long time ago, never used it though," she explained, "and you make me feel like an outsider when you smoke, so I thought I'd join you."

He cracked a smile and did a cheers with his cigarette which she returned.

"You seem a changed man since I met you, Steve, and yet it has only been a week or two."

"I feel changed, probably your fault, too."

"So did you get the job?" she asked and looked at the mailbox at the end of the road.

"I only just mailed my application."

"Well go look if they responded!" she urged.

"I just said, I've only just mailed the application."

Danielle got up, full of positive energy, and she dragged him with her. He did not mind, seeing as her mood was affecting him as well.

"Open it!" she said in excitement. Steve stared at the public mailbox.

"I can't," he argued.

"You haven't tried! Come on man!"

He indulged her and gently tried to open it. To his great surprise it opened up, though instead of being filled with mail, including the tube containing his drawing and application, there was only a single letter lying in there. It was a large brown envelope and it was addressed to him.

"You have got to be kidding me," he said in amazement, and felt as though he would never doubt Danielle again.

"So did they accept you?"

Steve did not open it, he did not have to, he knew they had. Instead he caught Danielle in a tight embrace, for the moment not doubting her physical presence.

"Careful soldier," she said, when they were once again standing face to face. "Don't want people to see you hugging the air."

He was about to answer when a voice called his name, they both turned around and saw a man walk towards them — well, toward Steve.

"Hey, Steve, long time no see," the man exclaimed and shook his hands.

"Hi, Khane, how are you?" Steve answered, even though he did not really feeling like chatting with Khane, who was an old college friend.

"Khane?" said Danielle "I used to have a sort of pen pal named Khane. He was from Australia," she contemplated.

At the same time, Khane responded, "Oh, not too bad. Just got a promotion here last week, so I'd actually say I was doing great."

Steve tried to keep Danielle's voice out of his head, but she was a tough one to fight.

"How about you?" asked Khane.

"Yeah, I'm pretty good," answered Steve, wondering if it was a lie or not, in the end he decided that it was not. He was doing pretty well, after all.

"You just got an awesome job, you're more than pretty good!" commented Danielle.

"Good to hear, good to hear," said Khane and patted his shoulder in a brotherly way. "Anyway Steve, I've got to run, I'm in a sort of hurry, but we should catch up over a cup of coffee sometime."

"You don't really want to talk to him, though," said Danielle.

"Yeah, that would be nice," answered Steve, and shook Khane's hand again before he left. "You're a pain," he said to Danielle and went back to sit on the staircase again.

"Oh, come now, Stevey Levey, open the envelope."

"Please don't call me that again." He started to open the envelope, though in the middle of doing so he looked up and said, "You know, it might be nice having a chat with the fellow, he really was a good friend in college."

"You just want me to be wrong, don't ya?" she

suggested with a smile on her lips.

"Well, it would be nice for once." He pulled out a bunch of papers and froze while looking at the first page. "This is a really good deal." He said, staying fairly calm.

"It is, and it's yours, little romantic. Give the dream a try, eh?"

"What are you?" He asked again still looking at the papers.

"I'm what I always wanted to be, the happy character with all the answers."

And when he looked up from the papers again she was gone. He smiled and whispered a quiet, "Thank you."

The following Sunday afternoon, less than 20 hours before he was to start his new job, he took Sarah for coffee and a walk in the park. She seemed to really enjoy it, though she did not say so. Steve was okay with that, though, he knew he could not change who she was, and after all, it was her he wanted.

After having been to the nearest Starbucks to get coffee, they settled on a snow-covered bench to talk. Here he told of how he had gotten fired, met a young girl named Danielle who had helped him, and of his new job with this grand old company. He left out the part about the speeding-ticket, also the fact that Danielle might in fact not be real. She smiled all the way through his story and did not interrupt him once. His romantic heart filled with joy at the sight of her. Good thing she was not the jealous type either, it was part of her calm charm and he could not help but wonder how this feature could have bothered him in the past. She seemed perfect, so very far from empty. In fact, he did not feel empty at all, anymore, quite the opposite.

At the small lake not far from the lovers, stood a young woman dressed in a long black coat, with her hands in her pockets, surrounded by ducks. She was out of hearing range, yet she knew what was to come, even if the lovers themselves did not.

"You guys were right," she said, looking down at the ducks. "I am *the* duck."

Penance

by Arnold Cassell

Once upon a time there were three teenage friends. Their names were... well, forget what their *real* names were, because they were going to a Renaissance Festival. For the day, their names were Mercutio, Jaquelyn, and Horrace. Mercutio was fairly short, blonde, and dressed as a bard. He had just learned a few tunes, and so he carried with him an acoustical guitar. He had the heart of the fair maiden Jaquelyn, who had the slender appearance of an elf. She had even braided her long red hair, and it lay beautifully on the soft green shoulders of her lengthy dress. Horrace was Mercutio's brother, and, though younger, Horrace was taller and broader. His voice was as low as his chest was wide, and they all three liked the way it sounded in duets with Jaquelyn.

They saw many wonders that day: sword swallowers, flame jugglers, card magic, and gymnasts young and old. Some of the comedy acts they had seen time and again for so many years that the three of them had memorized each gesture and inflection, but the acts had become memories so beloved they found themselves returning to watch every time they visited.

They were visiting one of their favorite spots just after two o'clock: a hand made wooden bench under a twisted but beautiful old tree. Horrace had once said it was like the tree had curled up so just to hold people up off the ground, and maybe it had. At this moment, a woman sat on the bench with a harp and played a few soft ambient tunes, and a jester lay in the bow of an accommodating limb, tracing the harp's notes with a softly waving hand.

They sat and enjoyed her company for a while, taking shade close by, until she noticed Mercutio's instrument. She insisted that he play her a song, and after a polite refusal or two, the three of them joined together for a go at "If I Was a Blackbird." It was one of Jaquelyn's favorite pieces from her visits to the faires, and with Horrace in harmony they commanded the attention of more than a few passers by.

During the course of the song, the jester in the tree froze rigid for a long while, then moved suddenly to sit and fix his gaze upon Jaquelyn, as if he had been entranced. The look on his face, however, was not one of admiration so much as avarice. A plot had been hatched. No one noticed him leave, and it was just as well: no one would have believed he faded into the leaves.

A few more people were pressing in to hear the impromptu performance, not realizing the three friends were patrons, rather than actors, at this faire. Jaquelyn and Horrace tried not to heed nor encourage the extra attention, and sang facing the lady with the harp instead of the growing crowd. They did not notice the dirty beggar edging closer, shifty eyes darting back and forth, nor the bottle he nervously grasped. He whispered a few words into his hands and pulled off the cork just as the song neared an end. Jaquelyn's voice trembled and faded as she reached the last few words, which had a poignant and sweet effect. A few people clapped for them, and she blushed, unsure exactly why she had lost her voice.

There was a bit of awkward confusion, as some people tried to offer Mercutio tips, but he politely refused, or instead put them into the basket of the harpist. He did not notice Jaquelyn had suddenly sat down on the bench in despair, one hand on her throat, and another in Horrace's grasp. She seemed in pain, confused, and her eyes darted around wildly like she was lost. Jaquelyn quickly neared exhaustion with her panicked effort to speak, but nothing would come out, not even a whisper. Horrace could not tell what was wrong, but Mercutio knew instinctively the moment he returned his attention to her.

He knelt by her, and ducked his head into her direct field of view. He pleaded with her to look at him, and to please, please calm down. He told her he could feel her pulse, and she was going to faint if she did not slow down for a moment. Looking into his eyes did help a bit, but she was terrified that she had lost her voice so suddenly and so completely.

Horrace and Mercutio assured her it was only temporary, and it was probably due to the heat and the dust in the air. The two of them waited until she had calmed down enough to stand, and escorted her to get a drink of water at a stand around the corner. They all sat down at a nearby show, and she slowly drank, trying after each gulp to whisper just one word, but to no avail.

"I could have told you it wouldn't work" came a voice from behind them, but they spotted no one when they turned to look, only laughter and the fragrance of golden fields was left to them. The two boys looked to her to comfort Jaquelyn, but her eyes were scanning, hawk-like in a predatory gaze. She felt oddly more comfortable with the notion that she had lost her voice due to a prank than some freak accident.

"You," came the voice from a nearby stage. "You who have lost something precious." It was the familiar face of one of their favorite storytelling acts, but glossed and still, expressionless almost. "Go now to the West, or you will never recover it. Quickly!" He finished, but stood motionless, pointing to Jaquelyn. She hesitated only a moment before she stood, grabbing the boys by the sleeves.

But quickly as they could find their way West through the faire, its makeshift streets clogged then dotted by the participants milling through it, something else beat them to the destination. Something that moved unhindered by the crowd on the dusty paths: a bird flying overhead, a black crow with three white feathers.

The three of them slowed when they arrived at the Western-most corner of the faire grounds and looked around frantically. Something was out of place, but what? They had been here so many times, seen all of these stores, talked to each of these storekeepers, every place- *but that one*. Had that curtain always been there? It was no wider than a door would be, just between the rose peddler and the wax shop. Both of those stores were open air shops, so you could see the entire inside from the outside. So that curtain must lead... where?

No one seemed to be going in or out of the curtain; no one seemed to notice it at all. The two boys followed Jaquelyn as she rushed to it, pausing only briefly to reach out and touch it, as if to make sure she was not hallucinating. As they passed the curtain – *through it? around it?* – they entered a space unseen from the other side, and they tasted the sound of wind chimes, heard the dust on the shelves, and felt as if their eyes were in moth balls.

It was disorienting and other-worldly to be sure.

All manner of things were stuffed onto the shelves of the dimly lit store. Wind up children's toys from the 1950s, jewelry boxes with all manner of decoration, figurines that seemed to be made entirely of... *spider webs*? Mercutio touched one of them and it stuck to his finger and then dissolved. Moments later the black circular base it been resting on began to reform a new figurine thread by thread.

Statues by the door, incense which stung the eyes, dusty paintings in rotting frames, live animals in cages along one wall, blankets and clothing of any style, trinkets and baubles and rusty mirrors, all were packed into a space no larger than ten feet in either direction. They heard the clink of coin changing hand and saw a glimpse of daylight from the side of the room. The sudden bolt of sunlight blinded them to the jester's exit, even if they could have recognized him. They only heard the gleeful laughter of the strange little shopkeeper as he came back to the center of the store.

He added a coin to his pouch and more closely examined the necklace in his hand, while the three examined him. Maybe it was the darkened space, the haze from the incense or some other trick, but his green-grey skin and long, pointed nose and ears looked more realistic than any prosthetic they had seen. His fingers, though longer than a normal human's of similar size, bent adroitly around the silver circle as his sharp eyes focused on it.

"You can't have it. It's too late. It's been sold," he grunted as all the joy left his face. Jaquelyn was more stunned than the other two, but all three were silent. The merchant looked up at them. "Yes, your voice. You shouldn't have sold it off in the first place."

Mercutio stepped closer to the short little merchant. "Sold?" he exclaimed. "It was stolen! We had no part in this, whatever this is, you little thief." He found himself at a loss for words, everything seemed so unreal.

"Stolen? You didn't sell, barter, or trade it to young Ilth?" asked the merchant. At the mention of his name, a pile of rags edged closer, grinning and nodding his head, as if to encourage them to say yes.

"No we most certainly did not!" Mercutio belted out, emboldened. The merchant turned to Ilth. "An extra two years then, for you. And this doesn't count towards re-paying your debt." The tattered beggar deflated and slouched down again, familiar lines of disappointment etched deeper on his face.

"Regardless, it has been sold at a fair price to a willing and worthy customer. I can't *un-sell* it," he almost choked on the word. "But if I could interest you-"

Horrace stepped forward and tried to use his height to intimidate the odd little man. Instead the merchant snapped his fingers and the statue by the door animated. A meaty hand roughly the size of Horrace's head fell on his shoulder and assured him he was out of his league.

Unfazed, the merchant put the necklace in a glass case with a few others and began his pitch again. His sales technique would have been perfect, if his potential customers had not been so infuriated.

"Where did you sell it? Who did you sell it to?" Mercutio demanded, trying to wrap his mind around the questions he had just asked.

Jaquelyn did not wait for answers; she darted to

the side door, and Horrace and Mercutio quickly followed. "Wait!" tried the goblin, following them to the curtain. "Are you sure I couldn't interest you in..." his voice trailed off as he realized he didn't have anything they wanted. He laughed a little at their misfortune, since they were no longer potential customers. He tried not to notice the rattle of the glass case, and the flutter of the other curtain. He focused instead on coldly calculating his gains.

Somehow the three of them were at the other end of the faire again, close to the food stands and the benches, back in the human realm. Jaquelyn was distraught and somewhat ashamed that she had expected to be elsewhere, but *where*? Neverland? The Shire? She sat down slowly at a bench, her head swimming with emotion and incredulity at her predicament.

Horrace and Mercutio scanned the crowd for a time, but neither had a clue what they were looking for. Jaquelyn began to cry, and at that moment Horrace noticed an outstretched hand reaching for her face. He seized it by the wrist and lifted the tattered little beggar into the air.

"Please, please! Don't lose them! He'll want them; they will fetch a high price." Before Horrace could strike the sad ball of dust and dirt, the beggar offered the necklace from the shop. "I'm here to help."

Looking into the desperate face of the pathetic (and somehow not quite normal) figure, Horrace could not help but be embarrassed by his rash action. The beggar introduced himself as Ilth, but quickly returned his attention to Jaquelyn. He collected her tears in a small glass jar. "Tears of despair, and very pure. You'll need these to bargain with."

"Bargain with whom? What are we dealing with? Who are you?" Mercutio asked, trying to put sense to the afternoon's events and comfort Jaquelyn. The four of them settled around the table and had a conversation that, at any other moment anywhere else in the world, would have landed them in a white padded room.

"He's a lost traveler. A traveler to other worlds." Ilth's voice took on an awed and wistful tone, and he paused for a moment, lost in consideration of a life that was not his. He quickly returned to himself and continued. "You see he's lost, and-"

"We caught that." Horrace interrupted. "Who are you, and why are you helping us, if you *are* now trying to help us?"

"Ilth. I was once a student of magic, but I, I made a terrible bargain. *My* story is unimportant, though." Ilth shifted uncomfortably on the bench. "Suffice it to say, not many folks go to goblin markets when things are going well. I'm indebted now, and I probably will be forever." Ilth's voice quavered a bit at the admission of his likely fate, and it softened the two brothers who moments before were ready to pound him to dirt. Or pound the dirt out of him. Hard to say, really, which would have been more likely.

"A *goblin* market?" asked Mercutio.

Ilth nodded persistently. "Goblins have a particular knack for finding a market for anything. They sort of, prey upon the weak, if you will. They know where and when to show up to fetch the best prices for whatever they have to sell."

"But we weren't selling anything!" Horrace's fist pounded against the table in frustration. "We were robbed! By *you!*" Horrace said accusingly and glared at Ilth, leaning closer as anger flashed in his eyes once more. The spell of sympathy for Ilth had been broken.

"Ilth raised his hands in a gesture both defensive and pleading and gushed his argument. "But this is a good sign! A helpful omen! Listen, the customer here isn't you, any of you. It's the traveler. You see? He's worse off than you are."

"I- we- " Mercutio stammered, trying and failing again to come to terms with the situation laid before them. Jaquelyn understood better then the boys, perhaps, but she could not speak to explain. A sigh of the wind eased across the table, and Ilth's eyes widened in terror. Without explanation, he bolted into the crowd, leaving behind the small vial and the necklace.

Jaquelyn picked up her tears and the trinket and stared at them for a moment. The two boys watched her and waited. Jaquelyn insisted, as best she could, that she was alright, and that she had a plan. Mercutio and Horrace helplessly followed her back to the strange curtain, but the goblin did not seem to be interested in the tears. They were careful not to show him the necklace, and he was careful not to ask them about it.

They returned to their favorite tree and sat in the sun for a while. Suddenly Jaquelyn's ears perked up as she heard a voice, *her* voice, singing in the tree behind her.

It was the jester from earlier, lying in the tree, on a different limb, this time, facing the sky, taunting them with his new prize. "Such beautiful music," he laughed.

Jaquelyn leapt to her feet, clutching the

necklace in her hand, burning with anger, but it abandoned her as quickly and completely as her voice had done earlier. The necklace was burning with her fury, but Jaquelyn was calm. She stood, stunned, for a moment unable to understand.

Horrace advanced, grabbed the necklace from her slackened hand, and leaped upon the diagonal trunk of the twisted tree. His anger continued to blaze as he half-stalked half-climbed the trunk to grab the lounging jester by the collar. "Is this yours?" he shouted into the jester's amused face. "Did you think it a fair price for her voice? Her song? Her, her goddamned *voice*?" Horrace was so mad that he could not think of anything else to say. He shook the jester by the collar instead.

But Horrace didn't stay angry for long.

"You DARE..." was all the jester growled before he began to transform before Horrace's eyes. His mouth grew wider and filled with terrible sharp teeth. His ears extended backwards into sharp points. His porcelain white face smoothed to the texture of steel and his eyes grew a razor edge spark to them. The sky seemed to darken around him, and Horrace was dwarfed by the power he now tenuously clutched in his hands. Fear gripped him, but only for a moment. The necklace quickly chilled in his forgotten grasp, and Horrace's fear was gone. He was left empty, confused. In his befuddlement, he surrendered hold of the jester-turned-monster.

Mercutio saw what had happened to his friends, how they remained motionless and dazed. No one but Horrace, however, had seen the transformation of the traveler; *that* was a vision that would haunt only him. Mercutio rushed in, up the trunk of the tree to his brother's side, and, after a few frustrating moments spent fumbling with the red tie that kept Horrace's sword in its scabbard, drew forth the sword with a clumsy flourish of triumph.

With a flick of his arm the jester summoned a rapier *from thin air* and bowed respectfully. Mercutio was shaken a little by his opponent's calm confidence, was shaken a bit more by his opponent's impressive sleight-of-hand, but found himself bowing in response. Mercutio had little idea of how to actually use a sword, but thankfully he was on equal footing with the jester on that issue.

By this time Jaquelyn and Horrace had recovered recovered themselves, and Horrace called out Jaquelyn's name.

Mercutio was startled, and looked to her. The jester mercilessly seized on the distraction and stung Mercutio on the wrist with his blade. Mercutio scowled back at the jester indignantly, but then half dropped half tossed his sword to the ground and went to Jaquelyn's side. "Blood of a hero," the jester murmured to himself, holding a vial to the tip of his sword. Once the vial was capped securely, he turned his attention to the two lovers.

Horrace caught the look of envy crawl across the jester's now normal enough face before a sigh replaced it with a mask of determination. The jester snatched the necklace from Horrace and walked to the bench to dangle it above Jaquelyn and Mercutio. It began to glow a brilliant gold, and their expressions faded from those of lovers at a passionate reunion to those of distant cousins at a family reunion.

Horrace was beginning to understand, and so he cried out, "Have you stolen their love as well? What is this necklace you-"

"Only an ounce of it, only an ounce," the jester interrupted as Jaquelyn and Mercutio stared in confusion at one another. "Their love, her anger, your fear, it will all return in time."

"And her voice?" Horrace asked. The jester took something from a pouch in his belt and held it up, idly regarding it in the late afternoon light. "Give it to her, then." Horrace pleaded.

"Very well." The jester grabbed Jaquelyn by the wrist and turned her to face him. "I will return this to you, that which I have purchased at a great price, if you promise me one more thing." The desperation on Jaquelyn's face was answer enough. He unstopped the vial and spoke a few words in a language the three did not understand. A warmth and light flowed from the unsecured glass to her throat, and she giggled at the sensation.

She was so delighted at that she threw her arms around the jester, but even that elation left her and fled into the necklace, so she stood there awkwardly holding her arms around the stranger's neck.

"That was all I needed," he said, gently shrugging off her arms.

Jaquelyn stared at him for a short eternity, and he could not avoid her gaze. He stared back, unsure who was studying whom.

When she broke the silence at last, the strength and surety of her voice and her words startled everyone. "You have played us all." Her voice lacked anger or warmth. "I don't know to what end, and I don't know who you are."

"A traveler. A lost traveler," the jester replied, sadness tingeing the edge of his voice. "But you have given me the key I needed to get home at last," he replied frankly, keeping any hope he might have felt held at a distance, lest then necklace take the long-awaited prize from him.

"Unwillingly." Jaquelyn added. "It *is* only fair, in this situation, that you should ask permission. And since you didn't before, you must ask now."

The jester could find no argument against her, and instead quietly replied, "I had hoped you would not notice, but I suppose without anger or joy to blind you, there was a risk that you would." He winced a bit, but then smiled broadly as a teacher might towards a star pupil. "How very perceptive of you."

"How long have you been lost in this world?" she asked calmly.

"One hundred and seven years," he answered, the truth of it lending weight and dust to his voice.

"Then I will give you permission to use your magics *only* on one condition. You must spend ten years more here before leaving, and it must be spent in service, to teach you some humility and respect for us humans." She intoned his sentence with a calm air, handing him the vial of tears.

He wanted to argue. He wanted to squirm out of it someway. He wanted to whine 'It's not fair!' but that would not have been true. *I do respect the humans*, he thought. But in her eyes he could see the truth, that it was only envy that he felt, which was not respect at all.

He stared at Jaquelyn, at the brothers, at this world, and accepted his fate. He bowed low to her. "I am bonded to your words."

Jaquelyn's love for Mercutio returned within a few hours, slowly at first, but then as strong as it ever had been. All their emotions returned before the end of the evening, and they found it hard to believe they had been without them for a time. But they were laughing and embracing as they left the faire that day.

"So it's done then?" asked the short, angry goblin as Ilth appeared through the curtain again. Ilth only nodded silently in response. "I should add another three years for the theft of that necklace," he threatened. But he felt the weight of the jester's gold in his pouch again, and surely forgot to follow through.

Robbery

by Michelle Herndon

Vampires are inherently creatures of the ground. Associated always with the earth in which they were buried, they are also extremely territorial. Good hunting ground is hard to come by, and once claimed, most vampires would go to any length to keep it. Sometimes their bond with the earth ran so strong a vampire could never leave it. They had to carry it with them, a constant reminder darkening their footsteps. When their forms shifted into that of whatever beast, they ran on all fours, close to the ground, salting the earth with their passing.

But Card liked to be above his surroundings, in height if not in metaphor.

All around the city spread out beneath him: an endlessly black sea on which floated tiny pinpoints of light. Currents of traffic coursed gold and red, as clogged as a city of this size's arteries would be.

A predator's perch.

It was a city of scents. There, on the wind, a complex collage of garbage, human filth, hot fumes, rotten food, and decaying flesh. A stagnant, toxic mess of waste left out in the summer's humidity to disintegrate into the ground. That so-precious earth.

At least up here, it was possible to find brief respite from the stench when the wind died. Then it was quiet. It was still. The sounds of the city muffled so far below they may as well have been from another world.

But, inevitably, Syd had to open his mouth.

"Which would you rather be? A rubber duck or a wind-up pink rabbit?"

Card enjoyed the rooftop perch and the serenity it offered. A good view without being seen. A perfect vantage point to sort out what valuable pieces of information the cityscape had to offer. It was only when Syd came up with these abrupt suppositions that Card began to calculate the odds of tossing him over the roof's edge and onto the sidewalk thirty-some stories below.

Card would have sighed heavily, if he was still in the habit of breathing.

"Is that relevant to…anything?"

Syd set his chin in one hand.

"I'd go with the rabbit. At least then you're mobile."

Card set his hands in his coat pockets and looked out into the wind, determined not to provide Syd any encouragement.

"I sure wouldn't wanna be a rubber duck. Can you imagine that? Having to watch the same person bathe every day for their entire life? Gross!"

Card's eyes narrowed. If only people bathed every day.

"Besides, even as a wind-up pink rabbit, I could still play my drums."

"This is why you're not allowed to get bored," Card rumbled. "You devote too much thought to these sorts of things."

"I only come up with them because I *am* bored," Syd pouted, and shifted his chin to his other hand. He crouched on the roof's edge, a squat complement to Card's tall, stationary guard. "How long have we been sitting here?"

"You've been sitting. I've been standing." The reflective sheen of Card's sunglasses tilted down towards Syd. "If you have something better to do with your time, then by all means—"

He stopped, abruptly and suddenly, his posture snapping to rigid attention like a well-trained dog. Card left the rest of his words unspoken as he turned his face back into the wind. He tilted his chin up, drawing in a deliberately slow breath between parted teeth.

Syd blinked at the change. "What is it?"

"Blood," Card growled.

It was faint. The merest hint of it on the air. But it was enough.

Syd stood up and brushed down his jeans. "Well, go on, then."

There was no effort in the movement. No planned path of thought beforehand. Card took off into the night, at one with the black. He darted across rooftops as the fleeting impression of a shadow, not even the sound or mark of a footprint left to indicate he had been there. He had found his trail, and no distance or persuasion of gravity would deter him from it.

Card was a hunter, and the epitome of the very ideal.

Syd watched him go, hands in the back pockets of his jeans as he chuckled a little and shook his head.

"You'd think he was afraid of missing something."

He took the stairs.

The scent led Card ultimately to a small, all-night convenience store on the outskirts of the city. A bastion of bright light when all the surrounding buildings were dark, it shone like a beacon in the night. A radiant bug zapper, drawing all manner of insects helplessly to it.

Only three cars were parked in the front lot. One of them rested beside a gas pump, its owner smoking as he fed the vehicle its oily dinner.

Two other humans were inside. One behind the register. The other browsing the aisles.

Card landed soft as a breath on a rooftop ledge across the street, safely beyond the radius of light the gas station produced while still able to pick out the images of the humans moving beyond the large glass windows.

His attention fell on the man browsing the aisles.

Card slid his tongue across the sharp press of fangs in his mouth, hardened by the scent of blood. It burned stronger here, but still muted.

It was somewhere inside.

Card swept his senses over the scene to take in what details were to be had. Things a lesser being may have never even noticed. The spread of flat oil stains peppered with cigarette butts gleamed with faint rainbows in the artificial light. The stench made the air thick and heavy. The oil stains were criss-crossed with the comings and goings of tires whose pattern and direction may as well have read like a script for who had been there, and how recently. The broken door of the station's external bathroom hung slightly ajar, allowing the flies free access to their paradise of filth and putrescence. A trail of toilet paper lay tangled in the weeds lining the cement blocks of the building's foundation, wet beyond use. Graffiti on the walls proclaimed the surrounding territory as belonging to this or that gang.

Humanity at its best.

The one filling up his car shut the pump off with a heavy clang and put the gas nozzle away. He turned, circling around the vehicle, and added the useless end of his cigarette to the mosaic of many already littering the asphalt. Then he climbed in and drove away.

Card stood in the smoking trail left in the car's wake, the expressionless sheen of his sunglasses turned to reflect the red glow of tail lights. He waited until the car had turned away on down the street before shifting his stance. His face tilted up, for a moment mesmerized in watching the moths and other nocturnal insects flutter around the fluorescent lights over the gas pumps.

All was quiet.

The scrape of his boots against the pavement reigned the only sound as he went inside.

The swinging door banged shut behind him with that particularly annoying beep of a warning system to let the convenience store employees know someone had just entered or left. The sound was jarring. Sudden. The man browsing the aisles had not been expecting it. Already tense and jittery with nerves, the gun he was holding went off, scaring both man and cashier alike with its thunderous explosion.

An innocent bag of charcoal stacked off to one side lost its life that night as its black guts spilled out onto the floor.

It did not take Card much longer to comprehend the situation.

The man's hand was bleeding. A glass bottle of alcohol lay shattered on the floor a few steps away, jagged pieces of glass tipped with red. A perfectly good ruse to draw out the cashier from behind his protective cage of bulletproof shielding. Card quietly nodded in a spark of admiration. It took dedication to willingly spill one's own blood over something as simple as a robbery. That earned the man a modicum of respect.

The cashier? Well, he really should have known better. A city such as this played host to all sorts of petty crimes. In nights where the strong preyed on the weak and kindness was rewarded with cruelty, he should have expected to be met with a gun in the face for his effort of rushing out into the aisles with a first aid kit.

Card smirked as the sound of the gunshot receded, leaving the two humans stunned in its echo. They had probably never heard the sound of a gun fired so close.

As for Card, it was a sound as familiar as a heartbeat.

Though, perhaps, that was not the best of analogies.

He shot forward with a speed neither human could follow. In one flawless gesture he yanked the gun from the man's hand, struck him across the jaw with the pistol butt, and thrown the cashier back against the nearest aisle. Hard. The cashier collapsed to the floor in a pile of packaged chips and string cheese. Card ignored the cashier and his groans. Instead his free hand snatched hold of the front of the robber's heavy coat and lifted him up off his feet, like he weighed nothing.

Card was not one for wisecracks. That was Syd's area of expertise. In retrospect, Card might have wished he had been able to think of something smart to say as he held the pathetic would-be criminal there at his mercy, glaring into his eyes through the tinted sheen of his sunglasses. Something to catch him off guard, or perhaps be viewed as a great irony by anyone who chanced to eavesdrop. But there was no one to hear.

He sufficed with the usual: a leering smirk, sparing the man no amount of fang, and a low, animalistic growl from deep in his throat.

The man turned an appreciable shade of white before Card hurled him through the front windows of the convenience store. Glass shattered and fell in a crystal rain all around, catching and reflecting the sickly pale fluorescence in tiny flashes when the shards turned just right.

Card had already bounded after him before the man hit the ground. The man's yelp was pained, crying out as skin scraped against asphalt. He had just come to rest on the oil stains and cigarette butts when Card was upon him again, grabbing his jacket collar and lifting the man up to his knees. The scent of blood, thrown fresh into the air made Card's jaw ache.

"Wretch," he hissed, and bit down hard as he buried his face against the man's throat.

Windpipe crushed, he could not even scream.

Syd pulled up on his motorcycle and parked it with a dying sputter of the engine. Leaning its weight to one side on the kickstand, he turned his gaze over the sight of the convenience store, and had to roll his eyes skyward at the mess Card had already made.

"Can't take you anywhere," he mumbled.

He slipped off the motorcycle and stepped quickly and briskly across the parking lot.

"Card! Oi! Card, you crazy git!"

Card did not hear, too caught up in his meal. Or, more likely, just ignored him.

Syd reached out once he was close enough and grabbed Card's shoulder, giving him a rough shake.

"Oi, knock it off. You're gonna kill the guy."

Card tore himself free with a frustrated snarl and glared up at Syd. His tongue slid out to lick away the blood smeared across one corner of his mouth.

"That's the idea," he hissed.

Syd released him with a shove. The man lay on the ground where Card had let him go, barely conscious. His body gurgled and groped numbly at the pavement. The gash along his throat was not deep, but it was bloody, spreading wide and meaty from ear to ear.

It smelled good.

"First thing's first," Syd grinned, reaching up to pat Card's cheek.

Card smacked his hand away.

"The cashier's inside," he growled. "You can deal with him."

Syd's brow lifted. "You left him alive?"

Card did not answer. He turned his face away and adjusted his sunglasses.

Behind his back, Syd's expression promptly burst into a beaming grin and he threw one arm around Card's shoulders, squeezing tight.

"There, see? You're getting better. I'm so proud of you, Judy!"

Card promptly dislocated Syd's arm from its socket.

"Don't call me Judy."

"Touchy, touchy." Syd clicked his tongue and turned away, snapping his shoulder back into place with a wince. "Was trying to compliment you." He rotated his arm experimentally to make sure it still worked.

Card remained silent as Syd bent to pick up the gun where it had fallen to the pavement among the broken shards of window glass. Whistling and spinning it by the trigger guard, he stepped aside and into the building. The security alarm beeped as the door closed behind him.

The cashier was not hard to find, still crouched and whimpering among a swath of snack debris on the scratched linoleum floor. He jerked with a start as Syd crunched a bag of pretzels under one boot, and tried to scramble away.

"Hey hey hey," Syd soothed, and crouched down to his knees, putting them more at even levels. "Relax, boy ol'. Not gonna hurt you. Just wanted to talk a little."

The cashier could not have been much beyond his early twenties. He had that gangly, awkward look of youth still about him. Pimple-faced, freckled and wide-eyed. The fact his eyes followed every gesture Syd made with the gun as he spoke seemed lost on the vampire.

"Let's see. What happened here, you think? You just about got robbed, didn't you?"

The cashier stared, frozen and dumb, until Syd tapped his sneaker with the gun barrel.

"Didn't you?"

The cashier nodded.

"Guy pretended to cut himself. Had a gun. Demanded the money, right?"

The cashier nodded.

"It was probably a gang thing, don't you think? You know how kids are these days. Not proper, upstanding citizens like yourself who actually has a job." Syd laughed and slapped the cashier's thigh with the gun barrel.

The cashier whimpered.

"Nope. Just gotta go around and take what belongs to other people. Probably just gonna use the money for drugs or hookers or the down payment on their Honda. Stupid stuff like that."

The cashier looked ill.

"This the first time you've been robbed, son?"

The cashier nodded.

Syd did, as well. "It's scary, I'll bet. But don't you worry." He gestured with the gun perilously close to the cashier's face. "Me and my buddy out there are gonna handle this. Your job is to just do what you would normally do. Call the cops. Explain to your boss why the place is trashed. Make something up to tell them about what really happened. There must have been a rival gang member that started the shoot out, right? 'Cause, I mean, one guy picking up both of you and tossing you around like rag dolls, that's just crazy. Right?"

The cashier clenched his eyes shut and nodded. The first wave of tears squeezed themselves out.

Syd patted the cashier's head gently. "There's a good boy. Don't you worry. You'll come out stronger in the end. In the meantime..." Letting his palm rest among the cashier's thin blonde hair, Syd concentrated, letting his power flex. It only took a moment to reassign the cashier's memories according to what "really" happened, just to be safe. "Have a nice sleep."

The cashier slumped down in a pile of cylindrical meat products, out cold.

The security system did not beep as Syd left.

Outside, Syd reached his arms up over his head, yawning massively to stretch his jaws before flopping back down to his usual slump. He scratched the t-shirt across his stomach and ambled back to where Card stood, the would-be robber at his feet.

"This counts as our good deed for the night, doesn't it?" Syd mumbled, pausing to look down at the man on the asphalt. Blood still gathered on the pavement and stained his clothes in places, but at least Card had closed the wound. He would live, albeit uncomfortably for a few days.

Syd nudged the man with his boot. "We can leave him here for the cops."

"If you're not going to eat him," Card grumbled, "then yes."

"What's this fascination you have with wanting to kill every poor dumb bastard we come across? I still don't get it."

"Ridding the world of useless filth." Card's face adopted something resembling a smile. "Isn't that what we do?"

"We?"

"Predators. Getting rid of the weak, the old, the sick."

"Garbage disposal's more like it." Syd reached into the pockets of his leather jacket until he found a pack of cigarettes, and lit one.

"What makes you think he won't be back here tomorrow night, trying to pull the same stunt?"

Syd shrugged, exhaling a breath of smoke onto the air. "Anemia, for one thing. Jail, for another. If you want a third, I'd say the problem's pretty well taken care of if you're half as scary as you think you—"

"Daddy?"

It was a small voice. A barely-there whisper on the faint wind. But it was enough for the two vampires to pick up on as they turned in unison, attentions focusing on the rusted pickup truck parked in the convenience store lot. The vehicle had been sitting there, quietly inconspicuous, since before they had arrived. Now, even as they looked, two wide blue eyes stared back at them from a face peeking over the open window in the truck's front seat. Framing that face were two pudgy pink hands, pressed against the glass, fingertips splayed as wide as those eyes which did not blink.

"Daddy?" she whispered again, craning her neck to get a better look at the unconscious man splayed across the ground.

Syd and Card stared.

The little girl ducked back down out of sight as she realized she had been seen, though the sound of her whimpers still carried.

Syd and Card looked at each other.

The cigarette burned on.

Card's eyes flashed red behind his sunglasses.

"Who brings their child along on a robbery?" he snarled.

Syd shrugged and took the cigarette from between his teeth, tapping ash off to one side.

"Guess he couldn't afford a sitter?"

Card snarled again, a vile curse under his breath in a language most of the world had forgotten. Syd replaced his cigarette and started for the truck.

Card's hands, clenched tight around the gray warmers that covered them, remained stiff at his sides.

"Syd," he called after him, a mild warning.

Syd ignored him.

The first wails of sirens sounded in the distance, drawing steadily closer.

"Syd," Card said again. More deliberate.

Syd waved a placating hand.

"One thing first."

Card glared behind his sunglasses. "We don't have time for this."

"We're immortal, Judy. We've got time for everything."

He ignored Card's bristling and put out his cigarette on the pavement as he sidled close to lean his weight against the driver's side door of the rusty old truck. He folded his arms over the glass window where it was rolled up only half way, and smiled down at the little girl.

"Hi," he said brightly. "My name's Syd."

She didn't say anything, dejectedly curled up in the seat.

"Mind if I sit down?"

The girl lowered her eyes until they were concealed from Syd's view, lifting an arm to drag across her nose.

Syd jerked a thumb over one shoulder. "That your daddy?"

She did look up at that, and nodded. "Is my daddy okay?" she whimpered, a picture-perfect image to tug at the heartstrings of movie audiences everywhere.

Syd made a face, and reached up to rub the back of his neck. "Well, see, your daddy is...well, he's sick. He's not doing too well. We need to get him home and into bed as quick as we can. Do you know your address?"

The little girl nodded. She straightened with newfound resolve and proudly spouted out where she lived, down to the letter tacked on to the apartment building.

At least her parents had been considerate enough to make her memorize that.

"Okay," Syd beamed, and patted the truck side as he turned away. He nodded to Card, still standing over the girl's fallen father.

"You wanna carry him?" he asked, after relaying the girl's address.

Card's flat stare returned with a monotone: "No."

"Okay. Then you drive the truck."

"I will do no such thing."

"C'mon!" Syd exasperated, tossing his hands to either side. The sound of sirens grew closer. "We gotta do something."

"No we don't." Card tipped his chin up. "Leave them. The human deserves his fate."

"Mitigating circumstances." Syd moved forward to pick the man up from the ground, careful in his handling as he turned to lay him among the tarps in the back of the truck. "You gonna help me or not?"

Card did not move. Behind the safety of his sunglasses, his eyes slid across from Syd and the body he carried to the little girl, watching from the front seat. Then back to Syd.

"I don't drive," he rumbled.

Syd set the unconscious human down in the truck bed.

"You mean you never learned," he could not resist teasing. Wiping his hands off, Syd turned to find Card standing not an inch away from him, having made nothing so natural as a sound in his approach. All he could see was himself in the reflection of those black sunglasses.

"You look too conspicuous like that," Card rumbled. "I'll take him."

Syd grinned. "Good boy." He reached up to pat Card's cheek again, but Card had already moved, crouching on the truck's edge as he reached down and pulled the girl's father up over his shoulder. He stood and settled the human into place, none too gently. Silhouetted against the black sky from that angle, all Syd could make out was the red scarf and white skin. Black pools where his eyes should have been.

He cringed. "Try not to break him?"

Card made a low sound. A firm pronouncement of proper derision. "And you try to remember which side of the road to drive on."

This time Syd scowled.

"It's America that's got it backwards. Not me!"

"What about your motorcycle?"

"Eh, I'll be back for it. It'll be fine."

Card said nothing more, but turned and darted away into the night. Disappearing with the shadows. Stepping between the shades of black. His preferred method of travel.

Faster, definitely. Less noticeable. But Syd would stick to his physical vehicles.

At least then there was something to listen to.

"Okay, kiddo," he piped as he plopped down into the driver's seat beside the girl. The truck started with only a slight protest. "You like music?"

Syd's hand went immediately for the radio.

Half an hour of classic rock later, the truck squeaked to a stop outside one featureless, squat apartment building. Just one nestled in a block of near-identical others.

"And that, my dear," Syd hummed as he shut off the truck's engine with a flick of his wrist against the keys, "is why Led Zeppelin is the greatest band in the world."

The little girl stared at him, much the way she had the entire ride from the convenience store, with that look of an open-mouthed fish. She had ridden in the truck many times with her father before. Though she was still young and not privy to many things, she was almost quite certain driving a truck involved stopping when the light was red, going the same speed as everyone else around you, and driving on the side of the road with everyone going the same way.

Syd had done none of those things.

Though he had told some funny stories.

"So which one's yours?"

The little girl slid out of the truck and walked around to meet Syd near the front. Lifting her head, she pointed to a dark window near the top.

"That one," she said, "with the blue curtain."

Syd followed her gesture, setting his hands on his hips.

"Hmm. That's a long way up there."

The little girl pouted.

"I don't like the stairs. The super-tendent won't fix the elevator."

"He wouldn't have used the door anyway. Maybe it's best if no one sees what time you get home."

The girl blinked. "Huh?"

"Oh, nothing. Just thinking out loud."

He turned his smile down to the girl.

"Wanna go for a ride?"

The little girl made a face, appropriately suspicious. "What kind of ride?"

Syd crouched down beside her as he pointed up to the top of the building.

"I bet I can jump all the way up there."

"No you can't!" she gasped.

"I can too!"

"Nuh-uh!"

"Wanna see?"

The girl's eyes grew even wider, should it be physically possible, and she nodded. Syd reached out his hand. She took it, and with one gentle tug he lifted her onto his back.

"Hold on tight, now," he hummed, rising back to stand.

The girl giggled, linking her arms around his neck. She kicked her legs experimentally where his arms looped to hold them. "Okay."

"You ready?"

"Uh-huh!"

Syd crouched, readied his stance, and leaped.

And kept going, loosed like an arrow towards the moon. Up, and up, and up.

The girl shrieked the entire way.

They landed on the edge of the rooftop with a feather's soft caress. Syd's boots stepped precisely and surely as he dropped down onto the flat concrete spread, turning his face into the wind to clear dark strands of hair from his eyes. Also to get a look of the girl's exhilarated expression just over his shoulder.

"Told you I could do it," he smiled.

"Again!" The girl squeezed where she held him. "Again, again!"

He held up one parental finger. "Ah ah. One time per night."

"Aww..."

He set her down. Her limbs proved a little wobbly as the rush of adrenaline wore off, so he held her hand, walking her back to the roof's edge before he hopped up onto the tall cement lining.

"I'm gonna go open the window, okay? Just wait here a bit."

The little girl nodded, but still stood on her tip toes to see as much as she could over the roof's edge as he ducked over it. She jerked back when he reappeared only a few seconds later.

"Oh, and by the way." He touched her nose. "Don't ever try this by yourself, understand? It's dangerous." He darted back down.

The girl bounced on her toes as she tried to see.

"How can you do that?"

"I'm what they call a trained professional," Syd grinned. He appeared above the roof's lining again and this time reached across to lift her up, over, down into the open window whose narrow ledge he balanced on. "We can do these sorts of things."

"Can I be a trained professional, too?" The little girl looked up hopefully once her feet were back on solid apartment flooring. Syd slipped in through the window after her, closing it securely.

"Maybe," he nodded. "In a few years."

The room was dark, but the little girl recognized it. She recognized the odd shade of the blue wallpaper, the way it looked when the only light falling on it was from what filtered in from the streetlamps outside. She recognized the curved

162

shapes of the rainbows she had drawn on paper, cut out, and taped up in various spots to decorate the otherwise bare and cracked surfaces. She recognized also the slumped figure in the bed pushed up against the wall, his breathing deep and rhythmic as he slept.

"Daddy," she whispered, and padded across the carpet to him. She climbed up on the bed's edge and reached out for his arm, giving him as strong a shake as her tiny hand could manage. "Daddy, are you awake?"

Syd put a hand on her shoulder, drawing her eyes back to him.

"He's gonna be asleep for awhile," he said softly. His other hand moved to dig through his jeans pocket. "We should let him rest, huh? He'll be okay. He just needs to sleep."

"Okay," the girl mumbled, though her tone carried nowhere near his sense of certainty.

Syd smiled.

"It's gonna be up to you to look after him until then, right? Do you have plenty of food here to eat?"

The girl nodded.

"What about your mom? Is your mom here?"

She shook her head.

"Okay. In that case, can you make sure your daddy gets this when he wakes up?" He drew his fist from his pocket, and into the little girl's hand pressed a business card, accompanied by a large wad of wrinkled green slips of paper with old men's faces on them. "He's going to need this, and those numbers are how to get in touch with a friend of mine who can help him get better, okay? Can you make sure he gets these?"

The little girl took the offering in both hands. Messy blonde curls caught and tangled around her face as she nodded, and with a dutiful reverence went immediately to a small set of drawers near the bed and tucked the cash and business card away in the top drawer.

Syd watched her, nodding his approval. "Yeah, you'll be alright."

He turned to leave in a more conventional manner.

The little girl's hands reached out to grab his wrist in both her own, succeeding at least in stopping him. He looked down.

"Do you have to go?" she pouted.

Syd pressed his lips together, and bobbed his head. Once. "'Fraid so."

"How come?"

"Because that's the way things are. But don't worry, kiddo." He plopped a hand onto her head. "I'll be back to check on you."

"We can go for a ride again?" Her voice ended in a hopeful upturn, making Syd grin.

"Oh, yeah. Definitely."

"Are you Superman?"

Syd had to admit that caught him off guard. His smile faded and he tilted his head to one side, giving the matter some considerate thought.

"I never really thought so," he finally mused, shrugging one shoulder. "I at least hope I don't wear my Underoos on the outside. But I can totally see myself walking around with a big old S on my chest." He grinned down at the girl. "Whuddya think?"

The girl giggled.

"Want another story?"

"Okay!"

"Okay. Which one's your room? This one, here? You go get tucked into bed, and I'll tell you another one. How's that sound?"

"Let me get my jammies on."

"Great. I know this one story you'll love. It's about this guy, Joseph, who knew a lot about dreams."

The dawn was beginning to break, draining the eastern sky of its color, by the time Syd was done. In true toddler fashion, the girl had insisted on not falling asleep, asking for story after story until exhaustion finally claimed her with morning's approach. Movingly silently across the flat carpet, Syd tip-toed out of her room, closing the door behind him so it clicked securely shut.

"Superman," he chuckled to himself as he left, the same way he had entered.

Card stood waiting on the rooftop of the apartment building, tall and statuesque against the edge. In typical Card fashion his hands were in the deep pockets of his coat. His white face was an emotionless mask concealed by the black tint of sunglasses over his eyes. No part of him moved save his hair, blown by the wind.

"Don't do that," Syd said as he climbed up to meet him.

"Do what?"

"Stand there, like that. All you're doing is looking creepy and malicious."

"Then it's working."

"What is?"

"My plan to stand here and look creepy and malicious."

Syd laughed as he plopped down on the rooftop's edge, swinging his legs over the side with a carefree energy. Their gazes turned out over the city as they watched the sun come up, enduring the instinct to run and hide from the creeping light as long as they both could stand.

"If you keep this up you're going to go broke," Card said at length.

Syd lit himself another cigarette, taking more time to enjoy it.

"No danger of that," Syd dismissed airily. "Unlike certain parties which shall henceforth remain anonymous – Judy – I have an income."

"And a need for material possessions," Card huffed, disdain personified. "Don't call me Judy."

"Yeah, well," Syd shrugged. "Can't help it. You know me. Big softie when it comes to kids."

"I had noticed that particular character flaw of yours."

Card turned away first, the sunlight becoming too much for him.

"You stink."

Syd toasted to that with a lift of his cigarette. "Through and through, boy ol'."

"No. Really." Card lifted a hand, making a gesture of waving it front of his face. "You stink. Go incinerate that jacket. It smells like week old fish."

Syd laughed, and let him go. He stayed a little longer to watch the first breach of the sun create a halo around the corner of the building it rose behind. He reached out his hand, giving his cigarette a tap, watching as a particularly hearty gust of wind carried the ash away to land in streets and puddles unknown.

"Maybe Kansas was right," he mumbled. "We are all just dust in the wind."

Lil Red & The Baron
A Tale of *The Scorched Earth*
by K.R. Gentile

"Asimov's sideburns!" Lil Red swore past the several thin metal lock picks held between her teeth, as the tumblers slipped out of place for the fifth time. It was not that the lock on the wood and iron-shod door was that complex. She could defeat harder in her sleep, but this lock was proving most difficult… especially since her lithe form was hanging upside-down and by her knees from a loop of smart-cable attached to a rafter three meters above her. It had not seemed at all this tough when she was practicing it at home, but now it was infuriating her. Gravity just was not cooperating in the least! She hated when things did not cooperate, but at least she had tied her long red hair into a braid that was circled securely around her throat, giving her the appearance of wearing a collar and keeping it quite out of the way. She glared down at the floor for a moment, cursing the thin traces of copper wiring that connected the grid of pressure sensors in the main hall of the Brotherhood's Monastery-Fortress, and then eased the pick and tension bars into the lock for another try.

As she wiggled the pick gently, easing the tumblers into alignment, she wondered if The Baron had been right all along. "Stealth be damned!" he had snorted while cleaning the connectors on his armor's shoulder plate. "The Brotherhood of Steel understands only force, so force should be the route by which they be taught a lesson." But Lil Red had eventually won the argument.

She had left without him.

It's not like I left without letting him know, she thought to herself as she worked the last few tumblers. After all, she had left him a note detailing her entrance into the fortress proper and the path she would take through the various guard points and sensory systems. She had even marked convenient places he could move to as she made her way through the maze of security, coinciding with her time schedule so that he could be there to bring the big guns to bear if she got into a bit of a jam. A satisfying "click" came from the door lock. *Not that I'd need him*, she thought triumphantly as she replaced her picks and tools into her crimson jerkin and slowly eased the door open. Behind the door, fifteen feet away and facing the opposite archway sat the expected guard, leaned forward slightly, reading from a parchment book.

Reaching up, she grabbed the cable and smoothly slid her legs from the loop, reversing her position so she now faced the door right side up. Then placing a foot to either side of the doorjamb, she kicked off hard swinging backward on the length of cable. The swing took her up and then quickly reversed and she soared through the open doorway, using the cable to snap her up toward the next room's ceiling as it caught on the top of the doorjamb. At the sound, the guard turned slowly and then snapped out of the chair as he saw the door standing open, only to find himself driven to his armored knees as Lil Red dropped from her arc to land onto his shoulders, the smart-cable disengaging from the beam and retracting into the canister at her belt.

As she drove him to the floor, her legs locked in tight around his neck, squeezing hard. By the time he was driven forward onto his face, he was out like a light, thanks to the lack of blood to his brain. She gently untwined her legs from his shoulders and patted him playfully on the neck, lifting the heavy iron ring of keys from the hook at his belt. "Sleep tight, my stalwart monk. I'm sure the Abbot-Captain will understand," she said as she walked across the room to the next door. *See, Baron? No Problems at all!* She mused to herself as she sorted through the keys to find the right one to open the next door. It slid in and popped open without a sound and she pulled the door open--much to the surprise of the Guardsman reaching for the handle on to opposite side. "Okay… maybe one *small* problem," she said as she slammed the door in the monk's face, and scrambled to drop the heavy wooden siege-bar across the door.

"By the Sacred Code, that girl will be the death of me yet!" The Baron exclaimed as he burst forth at a dead run from the small concealed cave that served as their home, the crumpled parchment note drifting to the floor, knocked from the wooden table by the swirl of the edge of his crimson cloak.

"Okay… maybe it's a big problem now!" Lil Red admitted to the unconscious monk as the tip of the war-axe split through the oak door. She stood in the center of the guardroom, the door on either side barred. *But, by the sound of it, not for much longer*, she thought as she scanned the room for options. It was a small room, less than 4 meters wide by 6 long and made of stone and scavenged metal beam rafters. The roof of the room was vaulted and high, maybe six meters at the highest peak, with the rafters set at about three. "No windows or vent towards the ceiling. This could be bad," she said as she rushed to tear the covers from the metal oil-torches on the walls and douse them out one by one. Darkness might buy her a minute or two more, but in a room this small, there would be little room to run from the armored monks currently chopping their way through both doors. Then as the last torch flickered out, her eyes caught a small grate in the floor at the center of the room.

She dove toward the grate, her fingers quickly pulling it free and then running along the sides. "Damned faulty logic in designing this place, that's for sure!" she cursed as she measured it with her hands. "Less than a third-meter at a side. This is not going to be easy." Touching her own shoulders, she measured a little over a half meter. Wincing, she heard the bar on the inner door begin to split under the force of the axe-wielding Brothers behind it. "Well, we all do what we must," she said, grasping her left shoulder with her right hand.

The door gave way finally, the siege-bar splintering at last and the monks spilled into the darkened room led by Abbot-Captain Julian Carstairs. A flick of a switch on his helm and a sun-bright beam of incandescence arced through the room, spearing the fallen Brother face down upon the floor. The accompanying guards took their cue and soon several beams of light were searching the rafters above and all the corners of the small guard-post.

Behind him, Father Emilio of the Alloy Cross cleared his throat. "I see nothing, Abbot Carstairs."

Carstairs snorted, and flicked his helm light off as another guard relit the oil-torches. "I concur, Father Emilio, but someone *was* in this room. How else would both doors have been barred from the inside?"

Two of the Brotherhood monks were lifting their fallen comrade to a chair as he groggily came around. "Brother Collins, report." Carstairs growled at the awakening man.

The monk' s head lolled about as he tried to fix his vision on his commander. "I saw nothing Abbot-Captain. A sound drew my attention to the door, which had been opened. The next thing I knew I was being forced to the floor and throttled by something from behind. And then you were here, sir."

Carstairs drew the man's face to stare into his eyes. They seemed cloudy and unfixed, but not by any drink or drug that he knew. "You saw nothing, Brother Collins? Nothing at all?"

The monk hesitated and then spoke. "Only one thing, the limbs that grabbed me were red and longer than my own arm, with a grip of hydraulics. And there were only two, but I could feel the weight of the creature's palm across my shoulders forcing me down."

Carstairs stood and looked at Father Emilio, who was thoughtfully pulling at the thinning Van Dyke upon his chin. "This means something to you, Father?" Carstairs asked as he directed two monks to take Collins to the infirmary.

"Perhaps, Abbot-Captain," Emilio said in that annoyingly cryptic way the Priests of the Alloy Cross managed better than anyone else. "I have heard of

173

such creatures, barrow wights and other children of the Scorched Earth that might fit what Brother Collins described. Perhaps it was not so much a hand as tentacles that strangled poor Collins."

Carstairs looked in disbelief at Father Emilio. "Are you suggesting, Father, that some *creature* opened a door and attacked Collins without making a sound, and not the young girl that Brentwood here saw open the door in front of him?" Emilio's dark eyes locked to his own blue ones from under the priest's hooded cassock.

"I have heard, My Abbot, of creatures that can assume many shapes, some even a gelatin or mist form. Surely a human girl would not be out of the scope of such a creature's accomplishments?"

Carstairs acquiesced. "But, Father, why would such a creature enter this fortress when there would surely be easier prey in the township below the hill?"

Emilio nodded. "Implausible, yes, but as implausible as a young girl making her way to the center of a heavily guarded Brotherhood Monastery, and the only guard that notices her passage is taken out with the ease of a child? No. Better that we look for the beast that has made its home in this House of God." And with finality, Father Emilio turned and exited the room, calling over his shoulder as if an afterthought. "You will catch this creature and see to its destruction by tomorrow's eve, will you not Abbot-Captain?"

Carstairs looked after the priest. "Aye, Father, by tomorrow's eve. By God's will, it will be done as you ask." Silently he mused as he looked again around the room, his eyes glancing over the small grate in the floor and then quickly dismissing it. *Creature it may be. But should this prove to be a*

174

certain young girl that I have in mind, Father, things of an implausible nature are commonly her stock and trade.

Meters below the armored feet of Abbot-Captain Carstairs, Lil Red dropped into a wider cross-shaft at the bottom of the airway, her left arm hanging at an odd angle along her side. Bracing herself, she quickly slammed the left shoulder with force into the wall of the cross-shaft, popping the joint back into place with a wince and slight whimper. Slowly she worked the arm back and forth, regaining its mobility quickly. Then shuffling down the shaft a few meters, she lit a small pencil-flash and unrolled the hand-drawn map of the monastery. "Okay... I dropped down 4 meters, and then moved five east," she traced a finger along the map. 'Which should put me about... here." She frowned at the location, far too close to the main barracks-cells of the officers of the Brotherhood of Steel living here.

Silently she drifted back along the cross-shaft passing carefully under the airway she had passed through to get here, and then continued along, occasionally casting a glance down a side shaft here and there. Apparently, these cross-shafts provide ventilation to the lower ward of the monastery and luckily seemed to be a uniform meter and a half square. Each side shaft seemed to end at a large grate and fan assembly. Edging up to one of the fans, she could see that it was hung on the grate itself, and should swing up with the grating. *Good, that means I won't have to disable one of them to move it out of the way*, she noted as she again traced a path toward her target point and then smiled at her luck, realizing that moving through the shaft way actually made it easier to reach her intended goal. "And a single trip through the Fortress and past the check points would be easier than one in and one out again." She made notes on the map, marking a small x where an up or a side shaft touched a room, vowing to remember this little time-saving design error in the future.

Finally, after several minutes of trial and error, she found her way through the small maze of shafts to a storeroom conveniently just down the hall from her target. Carefully she eased the floor grate out of the way and slipped into the dark storage area. She listened at the door for a moment, but heard no sign of a patrol and lit her pencil-flash again. The shaft way short cut had placed her several minutes ahead of schedule, so she had some time to kill and she spent it nosing around in the boxes, pocketing some small items of interest here and there.

One lucky find was an ingenious little bow-pistol that could fold its arms to fit in a slim holster, generously included in the case. A closer examination of the bolts the weapon fired revealed heads which were quite long and could be loaded with chemicals, capable of sinking in through a joint in an armored target and injecting him with a drug of choice. She spent the next several minutes filling a brace of dart-bolts with the knockout toxin she normally carried for her blowgun and strapped the brace and holster assembly onto her right thigh, testing its pull and loading time a few times. As she was about to leave the room, she paused then grabbed two more of the weapons from the rack, stuffing them and several boxes of bolts into a slim back pack (also graciously supplied by the

Brotherhood). She would have to dye the holsters and pack to match the dark crimson of her "working" clothes later. Her larcenous need satisfied for the moment, she eased the door open and looked around the hallway, ready to drift into the shadows.

The Baron lifted the two Brotherhood monks like children and dragged their unconscious forms into the brush just past the checkpoint to the Monastery on the hill. He glanced down, carefully checking each man's pulse to make sure it was strong and steady. He felt no malice toward these men; after all they were simply soldiers doing their job, much as he himself had been at one time. No, it was their leaders within the Alloy Cross that were the corruption that seeped into the Brotherhood, guiding their misdeeds under the guise of moral and racial purity. Were his hands around Father Emilio's throat, the result would have been much different.

Satisfied, he divested the soldiers of their weapons, secreting them away in the thick thorny brush down the road from the checkpoint for retrieval later. As an afterthought, he returned to the checkpoint and disabled their ground car and telecomm sets, just in case.

Taking a moment, he rose to his full height and used the dim light of the moon to check the map that Lil Red had left for him, scanning the timetable. He allowed himself a chuckle, for as impetuous and impatient as the girl was, she was thorough to a fault. He quickly veered off the road and began to make his way to the west side of the Monastery-Fortress, and to the next intervention point on the map.

Abbot Carstairs strode into one of the many guardrooms of Cathode Monastery with purpose, feeling a certain burst of pride at the sound of several pairs of armored boots hitting the floor in unison. His eyes scanned the room and the group of warrior-monks standing at attention.

"There is an intruder in Cathode and we have been commissioned by Father Emilio to ferret her- *it* out. Friar-Sergeant, you may un-code the weapons locker." He walked around as the Sergeant quickly inserted his key-chip into the port next to the carbon-steel doors of the guardroom's weapons locker. They slid out and tucked neatly to the wall with a slight *hiss* of hydraulics.

"Small arms only, Sergeant. After all we don't want new windows in the hallowed halls of St. Cathode's, do we?" This garnered a short burst of chuckles from the brothers which stopped just as abruptly as Carstairs returned his gaze to the line of men.

"You are to perform a room to room search of this level of the fortress and leave no area, no matter how implausible it might seem, unchecked. If anything seems out of the ordinary, report it and kill it… not necessarily in that order. Any non-Brotherhood persons should be immediately detained under the utmost defensive conditions. If they refuse for any reason, shoot them. I will sort it out with the Father afterwards. You have full authority to enter any portion of this level."

He turned to the Sergeant, who was busily checking and handing out various power-guns, gauss rifles, and other side arms and weapons to the soldiers. Carstairs accepted a power-gun and slung it over his shoulder. "Now, split into teams of three, and you two men," he gestured at two of the more veteran brothers, "you have the honor of being my team." With that, he turned and headed out the door, stopping momentarily to add an afterthought: "And, if any of you encounter a young woman dressed in red, *do not* kill her. I want her brought to me personally for interrogation. The team that brings her to me will earn a reward of 1000 Gold Eagles."

Lil Red pressed flat against the wall as the door to the guardroom flew open, almost crushing her against the hard stone. "And, if any of you encounter a young woman dressed in red, *do not* kill her. I want her brought to me personally for interrogation..."

She cringed as the voice of Carstairs invaded the hallway and the warrior-monks began to boil out of the room. From around the door, she could see the back of the Abbot-Captain's head and fought the urge to draw her own power-pistol and crush it from behind.

Search teams headed in every direction, thankfully too busy hustling to their areas to be bothered with shutting the door to the guardroom behind them. *Hmmm,* she thought to herself, *for a kay of eagles, I might very well turn myself in.* She waited a full minute, just to make sure that there were no stragglers in the guardroom, and then slipped out of her hiding place and continued down the hall.

As she reached the end of the corridor, she knelt and quickly pulled out her Raffles, attaching the slim probe to the chip-lock of the door. She activated it and the small computer quickly drifted through hundreds of configurations until the right one caused the door to unlock quietly. Easing out the small bow-pistol she had just acquired, she loaded it and slipped into the room. Several seconds later, the record keeper inside was snoring peacefully on the floor by the small desk, and Lil Red was easing the small bolt back into her harness to be reloaded later.

Now the main task begins, she sighed to herself as she looked around the room at the wall racks of data chips. She moved quickly from one rack to the next, checking the document codes on each against the one she had memorized earlier that evening. Several frustrating minutes passed and she occasionally cast a glance toward the incapacitated record keeper as she disqualified each rack and advanced to the next. Finally, she found one that matched the sequence she was looking for and began removing the data chips, carrying the handful over to the scribe's desk. There she popped each one into the data inscriber, skimming the catalog of each. As she came across one she felt was important, she copied the contents onto a spare chip and dropped it in her carryall.

At last, she found the set she was searching for and went to work in earnest changing small entries and then covering her tracks with a few scribe tricks that she had learned long ago. She then copied the altered chip, added it to her collection and carefully replaced the data chips in the racks in the order she found them. She stood back and observed her work, then adjusted the rack, turning a chip or two, and then checked again and was satisfied that no one would be able to tell the chips had been touched at all. Next, she scanned the remaining rows, taking chips from a second rack, copying them as well and then replacing all but two.

After several minutes of work, she purged the data inscriber's log from the point she copied the first chip, patted the still-sleeping record keeper on the head gently, eased the door shut behind her and turned to stare down the lens muzzle of an armed lazpistol. "Clarke's Balls!" She swore as the warrior monk smiled and tapped his comm.

"Abbot-Captain, I have your intruder. Corridor five dash three, this level."

Julian Carstairs was back in the guard-post where Collins had been attacked less than an hour ago, staring at the floor as his men watched curiously. He paced across the floor from the door to the chair, measuring the distance. "A little over four yards, not a long distance but long enough to do without a single footstep being heard." He turned to Collins. "And you are absolutely certain you heard nothing except a sound at the door behind you?"

Collins thought hard, trying to recall everything up to his unconsciousness. "No, sir, there was a sharp noise, I turned, and then I was grabbed from behind and forced to the floor by... by the thing, sir."

Carstairs rubbed his chin, and then removed his command helm, examining the rafters above the table. "And you are quite sure that the sound came from behind you, and not from above?"

"Yes, sir, it was from behind. I had my directional sensors on, just as you taught us, so that I could monitor both sides of the room as I sat."

Carstairs looked up again, and then walked to the door, opening it slowly. There was no squeak or grind as the door swung freely. Then he scraped his boot heel across the floor at the doorway. "And it was not this sound?" Collins shook his head and Carstairs peered about the doorframe. Looking closer, he motioned to one of the other men. "Bring the chair." He climbed up, looking closely at the top inside of the doorframe, using a small pen-flash to illuminate a small series of scratches, their edges still gleaming fresh. He stepped out beyond the door, looking up and spotted the shining edges of scratches along the rafter, the one just below a circulation vent. Stepping back into the room, he mused aloud.

"It- the intruder, rather came in through the vent outside and somehow circumvented the lock on the door without triggering the pressure plates on the floor. The door swings easily, so it would not have set off Brother Collins's directional sensor. Then, it managed to cross a distance of just over 4 yards to pass over Collins's head and attack him as he turned." He rubbed his chin again and thought. "But how?" he looked to the men with a raised eyebrow.

Brother Tannerson, a younger Brother of the order, but known for his excellence at hand to hand combat was the first to speak. "Well, sir... leaping from the door over Brother Collins's head would be an impossible task for a human, but perhaps not for a Wight or some other creature."

Carstairs considered briefly. "But, Tannerson, it would have had to know that the pressure plates extended all the way to the jamb, and then would have had to drop down to land precisely and without a sound, and then make the jump from a standing position, all in the few seconds it took Collins to react to the sound and turn. It would take a creature with timing and a precise knowledge of this monastery's layout."

Brother Fisher, an older Brother with a bit of experience out in the wilds of the Scorched Earth looked up. "Perhaps, Abbot-Captain, it flew to the rafters just inside the door? It could have easily moved above the rafters and caught Collins from behind as he turned."

Julian looked up at the rafters again. "Perhaps. Tannerson, climb to that beam and check it for scratches as well." Tannerson reacted immediately, removing a folding grapnel and length of smart-cable from his belt and tossing it over the rafter. Tapping the cable sheath at his belt, the cable retracted lifting him from the floor to the rafter, where he deftly pulled himself up and searched. "No signs of scratches, fresh or otherwise, Abbot-Captain." He said as he lowered himself from the rafter and detached the grapnel, releasing the cable into its sheath.

Collins whirled around, his hand dropping to the butt of the lazpistol at his hip.

Carstairs's eyebrow raised as his hand also closed instinctively around his own powergun's stock, ready to bring it into play at a moment's notice. "Collins, what is it?"

Collins blinked, peering around the room. "The sound... I heard it again, just now."

Carstairs looked toward Tannerson and Fisher. "I heard nothing, Collins." The two other monks also shook their heads.

"I swear by God himself, Abbot, I heard the sound the creature made."

Julian swiveled about the room, looking up and around. "Collins... there is noth-" suddenly he stopped in mid-sentence. "Collins, close your eyes, and turn with your back to me."

The Brother looked a bit confused, but closed his eyes and did as he was ordered. Again the sound of the creature was there. His eyes flashed open and he spun, his lazpistol clearing his holster and pointing to the direction of the sound before his vision had even focused, only to find the muzzle of his weapon pointed directly at the Abbot-Captain.

The sound came again, and Collins looked hard at the Abbot and the movements of his hands pulling the smart-cable a very short distance from his sheath, and then releasing it with a snap as it suddenly retracted back into its housing.

Carstairs smiled. "The intruder used a smart-cable to pivot into the room as might a child swinging on a rope over a river, releasing just at the height of the swing to drop into the water. Or, in this case, onto Collins's shoulders." He turned, pointing out the scratches on the doorframe. "That's how the intruder avoided the pressure plates as well, hanging from the rafter below the vent by the very same cable. We're not looking for a creature... we're looking for a thief." *A very good and very bothersome thief*, Carstairs added silently as he walked over and replaced his helm. Tannerson spoke. "But, if that's true sir, then how did the thief get out of the locked room with Brothers at both doors?"

As he turned, Carstairs eyes drew again to the small grate in the center of the room. "I'm not sure, Tannerson, but I have a very good idea where the intruder exited." As he was about to investigate, a message crackled over their comms.

"*Abbot-Captain, I have your intruder. Corridor five dash three, this level.*"

"Hold her there, I'm on my way, and don't let her get too close to you!" As the men began to move quickly towards Grid Five of St. Cathode's, Carstairs grinned coldly. *A very good thief, indeed, but not quite good enough.*

The Baron stood close to the outside wall of the fortress-monastery, allowing himself to be cloaked in the shadows, hidden from the walking patrols moving above him. His eyes had adjusted to the darkness well enough that he could see every detail of the steep rocky hillside below him. Whatever disturbance was going on was definitely inside the monastery and not outside of it. *And, if I have any intelligence at all, I have a feeling I know what that disturbance might be*, The Baron thought as he referenced the time for the third time in as many seconds. *And behind schedule as well, I see. Gibson's Visions, girl… you'll be late for the Final Dismantling if you have your way of it.*

As he flipped through the various coded frequencies of the Brotherhood's communications system, one abruptly caught his attention.

"*…your intruder. Corridor five dash three, this level.*" The Baron drew out the map Lil Red had made of the Monastery. "By the Three Laws, what now?" he muttered.

As he moved into the moonlight, a voice came from above the wall. "You there! Step out where I can see you!"

The Baron swung his powerlance, the cannon-type powergun he carried, toward the sound and triggered a shot without looking, the whip-crack of the shot was followed by the thump of the armored monk landing on the other side of the wall. He squinted to magnify the small light-colored drawing, quickly finding the area of the map designated by the comm announcement. More voices replaced the fallen monk above and The Baron moved off quickly along the wall, trying to find the best entry point.

Brother Carlson was puzzled by the Abbott-Captain's response as he held his lazpistol on the red-clad girl. *How did he know it was a woman?* he thought to himself as he regarded her coolly. "Don't get too close?" he said aloud as he regarded his 1000 eagle prize. The woman was seventeen years if a day, short, slightly built, hardly a slip of a girl, wearing a hooded jerkin and pants of red leather. Yes, she had some interesting weapons on her belt, including, he noted, one of the Brotherhood's new bow-pistols and a small caliber sliver pistol. But he was an armored warrior with a charged lazpistol pointed at her head.

The girl smiled.

"So… come here often?" She asked, her green eyes twinkling as her red lips parted in a grin. The grin was infectious and he tried his best to stay stolid.

He failed miserably, and the grin broke on his own face. "Often enough to know I haven't seen you around. A bit young to be a training-brother, aren't you?"

The girl laughed, a tinkling light chuckle. "You never know, Friar Sergeant, they are making Brothers a bit stronger and more exciting every day."

She moved a bit closer, her finger pushing away a slip of long dark red hair that had fallen alluringly down across her left eye.

"Well, that they are. Oh, and I'm just a Brother, miss." Carlson was still grinning when a pile driver in the form of a red leather booted foot came up between his legs and into his groin, staggering him. As he bent over, two gloved hands locked in a vise behind his neck as the knee came up and crashed into his face. Carlson never heard her reply as he blissfully collapsed into unconsciousness, away from the pain of his crushed genitals.

"I know. You're too stupid to be a Sergeant," Lil Red growled as she let the Monk slide into a heap on the ground.

As she knelt to retrieve his lazpistol, a wave of heat brushed her cheek and the edge of her hood began to char and smoke. Looking up, she could see Brother Carlson's two teammates hustling down the hall toward her, one dropping to his knee, lazrifle ready to fire again. As she rolled, she snagged a canister off her belt and spun it toward them, the metal cylinder spraying a thick bluish aerosol as it rolled. Not only would the aerosol render the lazgun useless, the smoke would cover her dive down the intersecting hallway, which she did with amazing skill, coming up to her feet and into a dead run. As she bolted for the next intersection and the stairs that should lead up just beyond it, she set the liberated lazpistol from pulse to beam. The beam would not do much damage at first touch on a target, but the constant stream of energy could be waved around like a hose to catch several targets at once, giving her a chance to dodge an interception.

Lil Red rounded the corner and ducked as

splinters of shattered concrete sprayed her, the crack of a powergun ringing out from the stairway as its bolt impacted on the corner of the wall beside her. Waving the lazgun toward the stairs and grinning at the yelps of pain, she changed her course and headed in the opposite direction, hitting the door at the end of the hallway like a runaway freight train. As she rolled and came to her feet, she noticed a form huddling under the expansive wooden writing desk and a wide smile spread across her face. Grabbing him by his black robes she hauled him to his feet.

"Why, if it isn't Father Emilio! God still talking with the Church or has he finally written you guys off for the preening self-righteous fascists you are?"

The Alloy Cross Priest struggled to pull the vibro-dagger from his cassock, when the sharp stab of the lazgun's barrel in his cheek halted him. "I hope he's listening to you right now, Father, because if you don't drop that blade, I'm sending you to him without an advance warning."

The Priest swore and dropped the knife to the floor.

"You will not escape the Lord's vengeance of my death, thrice-damned harlot, even if you somehow escape the Brotherhood's."

Lil Red chuckled coldly and yanked him in front of her, twisting his arm up sharply into an arm lock. "But that's *exactly* what I'm going to do, Father, with your help of course."

Emilio looked back over his shoulder, as much as the gun wedged into his neck would allow. "And why on earth would I help you?"

Lil Red purred in his ear. "Because if you don't, then you're going to find out first hand on how indiscriminate the Brotherhood of Steel is with their friendly fire." Lil Red forced him out into the hallway in front of her.

Julian Carstairs rounded the last turn in time to see several Monks backing up towards the stairs. "What's going on here? Why are you retreating?" he demanded as he approached them. As he fell into the line of Brothers, he could see the figure of Father Emilio and another figure just behind him. Carstairs moved closer.

Father Emilio screamed. "Get back, idiot! Can you not see the weapon to my head? I'll have you flog-"

"Red. I knew it was you somehow." Carstairs shook his head, as Father Emilio's eyes bugged out in that ever so attractive way they did when he could not believe the truth in front of him.

"Carstairs, you know this, this-"

"Thrice-damned harlot?" Lil Red interjected with a grin.

Father Emilio snorted. "Abbot-Captain, you have acquaintance with this girl?"

Carstairs nodded. "Yes, Father, we have bumped into each other before."

Lil Red chuckled. "You see, Father, me and the Abbot here have danced this dance before. Before you came here, that is." Lil Red pushed the gun deeper against her hostage. "And I would think that by now he would know not to try that 'I'm going to slowly sneak up on her' crap. By the way, how's Father Barnhart? Still limping from that little oopsie with the powergun?"

Carstairs stopped as Father Emilio shouted,

"Are you insane, man? You are to back away right now Abbot-Captain. Do not be foolish with the life of a cherished servant of God!"

Lil Red laughed as she eased the priest toward the stairs. "A cherished servant? And here I thought all I had was a pompous, manipulative popinjay?"

Carstairs ignored the insult, silently damning himself for agreeing with her about Emilio. "Red, what do you want this time?"

"Just for you to clear me a path across the courtyard and to the east gate. And this time, no last minute heroics. Remember what happened last time you pulled something with me."

Carstairs grimaced and tapped his comm. "Clear the stairs and corridors two through seven, Level G. No one is to shoot at the intruder, she has Father Emilio as hostage." He looked over to Red. "Is that good enough, or do you want directions, too?"

Lil Red just grinned, taking the stairs slowly, Father Emilio clamped tightly to her. At the top she could see the other armed Brothers backing away. "Nope. Thanks for the offer, but I know the way."

I'll bet you do, Red, Carstairs thought to himself as he watched her move slowly up the stairs and out of sight. As she vanished from view, he tapped his comm again, switching to an unofficial channel that only a few Brothers even knew existed. "Abbot to Hawk Team, Crimson Gambit One. I repeat, Crimson Gambit One." Carstairs smiled a cold smile as he shoved past the Brothers in the hallway and mounted the stairs, following Red's path. *This time, girl, you will not get out of Cathode alive.*

Lil Red eased up the stairs and began to weave

her way toward the doors that would let her out into the east courtyard. At each turn, she could see the armed Brothers backing away, each one eager to take the shot with only the fear of Carstairs keeping their weapons at bay.

"You know something, Father?"

Emilio sighed. "I know that I am going to enjoy watching the Inquisitors rip the confession of your sins from your dying body, child."

Lil Red chuckled for a second. "Well, that's not exactly what I was thinking. I was thinking on how easy this escape is."

Father Emilio snorted. "What did you expect, young lady. You have a Priest of the Alloy Cross as your hostage. They would not dare chance injuring me to bring a common thief to her just rewards."

Red jabbed him with the muzzle of the lazpistol as they rounded another corner. "I'll have you know that I am NOT a common thief. I am an *excellent* thief. Quite daring, actually. And if you think that of Julian Carstairs, you are dead wrong, Father. He hates me."

Emilio gasped. "Surely you don't think that he would endanger me simply to get to you, arrogant girl."

"Hell, padre, he's the one that shot through old Barnhart with the powergun just to try to wing me so he could get a clear second shot. He *really* hates me," she chuckled as they rounded the last corner and the outside door came into sight. She called ahead to the Brothers there.

"Would one of you gentlemen be so kind as to get that door for me? I seem to have my hands full with this religious treasure." The Monks did as requested and they eased out the doorway and into the courtyard beyond. As they did, high intensity searchlights locked onto the pair, and the ensuing flood of artificial daylight illuminated the grounds. Emilio and Red shared the same whistle of astonishment at the sea of armed Brothers filling the stony courtyard. The sounds of weapons activating was a symphonic roar of clicks, clacks and whines.

Lil Red whispered closer to the priest's ear, "You see, I wasn't exaggerating when I said he really, *really* hates me."

On a battlement above the east courtyard, the Brother known only as "Hawk One" carefully opened a weapons case and began assembling his rifle. A lazgun set in the microwave range, this one had been designed before the Scorching as a special precision weapon with comp-assisted targeting and an electromagnetic aiming wave to help with dispersion avoidance. As he lay down, the hooded Brother affixed the adhesion bolts of the small tripod to the ledge of the tower and sighted in on the back of the crimson clad woman. He then made a subtle hand gesture. From two other battlements, the hand gesture was returned as Hawk Two and Hawk Three signaled their readiness. Never taking his eye from the scope, he tapped his comm. "Hawk Team is in position. By God's will and your command, Abbot."

Carstairs smiled as he heard the reply from his special surprise for Red, and stepped out into the glaring light of the courtyard. He changed channels on his comm to the monastery's announcement system and his voice boomed out of hidden speakers.

"Red, as you can see, you will never make it far from the grounds, nor with the Father leave them. Can't we be reasonable about this? Give yourself up and I will see to it that you are given a confessor to ready yourself before entering the kingdom of Heaven."

Lil Red chuckled and spoke to the priest clasped to her. "Hmmm, he promises me a *clean* death, *you* said torturing. Maybe I should just give up? After all, the Abbot is giving me the better option. Hell, he's even guaranteeing me a shot at Paradise."

Emilio winced. "Blasphemous witch! You will no more enter the gates of Heaven than the Dark Angel himself!"

Lil Red yelled out. "Sorry, Julian, but the Father here says I can't go the heaven after all. And if I can't go and look down on you guys burning in hell, then I don't want to go at all. I guess we'll stick to my first plan--walking out through the gates!" She caught Julian's cold smile from across the courtyard.

"Then, I suppose we will just have to play it by ear." He tapped the comm again and whispered into it. "By God's will and my command: Now." On the east battlement, Hawk One made the sign of the Alloy Cross and pulled the trigger.

Down in the courtyard, Lil Red screamed as the first maser packet hit her square between the shoulder blades.

Father Emilio felt the sharp burning as he found himself suddenly pitched forward, the girl falling on top of him. As he dragged himself from beneath her, he reached up to feel the cauterized wound where his right ear had been. He turned to see the girl crawling toward the fallen lazpistol when her side ignited into flames as another lazbolt tore into her, rolling instinctively as she screamed.

He crawl-ran toward Carstairs, screaming. "You bloodthirsty imbecile, you took my ear! You could have killed me!"

Behind him the girl rolled and fired wildly with the pistol toward one of the towers, but another lazbolt tore the weapon from her grasp, along with several fingers that vaporized when the bolt hit. Several of the Brothers ran toward Emilio, grabbing him and half-dragging him to his feet and out of the crossfire about to ensue. Even they wore bewildered looks as yet another shot tore into the crawling woman. As they approached Carstairs, Emilio brushed the monks away and began to admonish Carstairs when the east wall exploded. Through the flames, a huge armored figure strode as if unaware of the burning wreckage around him. Carstairs muttered a low curse.

The Baron had arrived.

The Baron had heard the command to fire as he flipped through the comm-bands. He stopped as he heard the first scream, and with a thought twin rockets leaped from his shoulder-mounted launchers to tear a huge gap in the east wall. A second volley annihilated the small gauss gun emplacement, raining exploding ammunition and flaming wreckage throughout the courtyard. As he moved through the cratered wall, his eyes locked on the energy flash from the east emplacement and he targeted his powerlance to spray several bolts of kinetic force.

The bolts sheared through the top of the tower and Hawk One died under the crushing wall of rubble that descended upon him. As he entered the courtyard proper, The Baron could see the looks in the eyes of the Brotherhood monks that surrounded Lil Red's still moving body.

The bear-sized armored warrior ignored the heat of the flames that set his cloak afire behind him, switched the powerlance's setting to full-auto and sprayed the firing Brothers, their lazpackets dispersing on the polarized crimson battleplate he wore, the gauss rounds bouncing off and the powergun shots barely moving him. His visorless helm tracked back and forth, coding targets to the smart-cannon's targeting system, letting the comp acquire and destroy targets by order of threat as he made a steady beeline toward Lil Red.

Another energy signature from a second tower caught his attention and a full volley of twelve rockets reduced the sniper and the surrounding battlement to rubble as they detonated. As another group of Brothers opened fire, his left hand extended and several auto-fed proximity grenades hurtled toward them, filling the air around them with hyper-accelerated shrapnel, tearing through their body-armor like bullets through tissue paper.

Emilio gazed in utter awe and fear as the massive crimson-armored warrior systematically ripped through the Brotherhood of Steel's troops, and then swung on Carstairs, who was already heading for the cover of the fortress itself. "By God, stop him Abbot. It's but one man. Destroy him!"

Carstairs snatched up the priest by his cassock. "A man, Emilio?" he spun the priest around to look at the carnage. "If the Dark Angel has a single general of his devil's army, you are seeing him! But I have something that may send him back to the Crevasse." As the priest watched, a Brother helped the Abbot lift a boxy ordnance launcher to his shoulder and his eyes opened wide as he could see the three warheads inside, each marked with the symbol of the Trinity.

Emilio grabbed the man's arm. "I will not allow this! You are not authorized to use micro-nukes except in the most extreme circumstances!"

Carstairs sneered at the Alloy Priest and his eyes blazed with an insane fire. He then spun and shot the Brother point-blank with his powergun. Spinning back on the Priest, Carstairs locked him with his maddened gaze. "And you, Father Emilio, just *order their use*. Do you understand me?"

Father Emilio nodded and tried to back away into the hallway, but the Abbot grabbed him with a gauntleted hand. "Speak... the... words... Father!"

Emilio stuttered them out. "I, Father Emilio of the Alloy Cross, authorize Abbot Julian Carstairs of St. Cathode's Monastery to use Trinity-Class Ordnance in the defense of his Lord's holdings. God's will be done." The ordnance launcher beeped cheerfully as the priest's voice-code unlocked its firing systems. "And God have mercy on your soul, Carstairs." He added as he backed away.

Carstairs grinned and fired the powergun into the priest's chest, killing him instantly. "And on yours, Father," he said as he stalked from the empty hallway and back to the firefight in the courtyard.

The Baron reached Lil Red and touched his gauntleted hand to her chest, detecting for activity.

She coughed and opened her eyes to gaze at him.

"What took you so long?" she asked, agony filling her voice, and passed out.

As he began to pick her up, using his own massive frame to shield her from stray shots, alerts suddenly screamed in his helm. "Trinity-Class Ordinance detected," the smart-comp blurted out, pinpointing the location on his sensor grid. The Baron spun on one knee to see Carstairs aiming the launcher from across the courtyard. The powerlance swung up firing as the small laser painter mounted on the launcher touched his chest and set off a targeting alarm. As the powerbolts slammed into Carstairs, the micro-missile leapt from its launcher and covered the short distance to The Baron and Lil Red. A white light exploded and engulfed the center of the courtyard. The monks found themselves blinded as environmental safeguards snapped on automatically in their armor. Those without armor were vaporized by the detonation of the micro-nuke. As their visors depolarized, many of the surviving monks stopped dead in their tracks.

In the center of the courtyard was a small crater, and in the center of that, surrounded by an iridescent globe of energy was The Baron, still kneeling over his charge. As the glow dimmed the crimson-armored figure picked up his fallen companion and calmly walked through the radiation zone and out the east gate of the monastery. Some brought up their weapons to aim at the giant, only to lower them again, realizing the inefficacy of any arms they could bear against him.

"And Father Emilio was killed in the blast?"

Cardinal Paolo asked, sitting beside the infirmary bed, his record-keepers taking notes as the conversation wore on.

A shattered, slightly electronic voice emanated from behind the curtain. "No, Your Grace. A stray round of powergun fire hit the unfortunate Father Emilio before I could get a targeting lock on the creature. There was nothing I could do to save him, though God knows I would have protected him with my life."

Cardinal Paolo gave the sign of the Alloy Cross at the mention of the priest's death. "I see, my son, and what of the creature?"

The labored voice again addressed the Cardinal, an odd counterpoint to the continuous *whoosh* of an oxygen pump somewhere in the unseen room beyond the curtain. "Vaporized in the blast, Your Grace. The barrow wight may have been born in the fires of the Scorching, but very little could have survived a point-blank detonation."

The Cardinal nodded. "Very well, my son. I find that you were not in neglect of your duties as Abbot-Captain of St. Cathode's Monastery. I understand that the medics say that they can have you back on your feet within the month. I would like you to return to your post, if you so wish it, Julian, although I will understand if you would rather not. You have sacrificed much for God, and he will understand your apprehension."

Julian Carstairs smiled painfully from behind the curtain, his face tearing anew from the movement, blood running freely from the healing radiation burns. The medic-comp fed him another burst of anesthetized oxygen through the tubes in his nose. Through his new eye, he could see the heat image of the Cardinal and his entourage on the other side of the curtain. "I would like that, Your Grace. After all, I am in the service of God. He has seen fit to let me survive this ordeal. There must be a reason."

"Then, by God's Will, I reappoint you Abbot-Captain of St. Cathode. And now, my son, I will take my leave of you. Please let me know when you return to duty so that I may assign a new Father to the monastery." The Cardinal reached toward the slit in the curtain to shake hands with the fallen soldier, but was stopped by his aide, reminding him of the loss of Carstairs's left arm. He had not healed enough from his minor radiation exposure for prosthetic limb replacements as of yet, as the doctor had informed them when they had first arrived. Luckily his armor had sealed the best it could when the micro-nuke detonated. Had it not, the monastery would have needed a new Abbot as well. "Good day to you then, and may God protect you, my son."

As the Cardinal left, Carstairs smiled through the pain.

Lil Red awoke, her time reference telling her four days had passed since the raid on the monastery. In the chair next to her bed sat The Baron.

"Was it worth it?" he asked as she opened her eyes.

She thought for a second and then nodded. "The supply and food shipments for the next quarter have been changed from protected Brotherhood camps to 'free' towns all over the area. It should be easy for the people to gather what they need before the Brotherhood realizes the mistake. And since each drop point is different, and they match the rosters in the record at the monastery, they won't know enough to change more than a few at a time. That should feed most of the people through the winter."

"And you covered this little change how?" The Baron asked, making a mental reminder to have the schedules dispersed through the normal channels.

Lil Red chuckled a bit. "I stole some records of pre-Scorch weapons caches that had yet to be raided by the Brotherhood. If we act fast we can gut more than enough to keep us in business for a very long time. Also, I copied some troop patrol assignments and made it obvious enough that someone tried to hide the data copy. They'll be so busy looking for ambushes and trying to get to the caches before 'The Resistance' does, they'll never think to look at the mundane stuff."

The Baron nodded. "How is the new hand?"

Red flexed her fingers a bit. "A bit of servo misalignment, but I can fix that easily enough. And you?"

The Baron stood. "I have a line on a new EM-Shield Generator. We were never designed to take a point-blank tactical hit, so the last one burned out after discharge. And you, girl, were very lucky. The snipers were using electro-magnetic enhanced microwave lasers, pre-Scorch hardware. If one had gone for a headshot, you would have been wiped clean. I still had to barter quite a bit to get your chest systems repaired or replaced." He paused for a moment and the turned to face her again. "By Rucker's Nano, girl... what were you thinking taking off like that? I told you we needed a bigger diversion. Now I see why we never liked to work with infiltration types, too independent and sneaky for your own good."

"Since when is an Armageddon-Class Warbot worried about working well with others?" Lil Red chuckled. "Anyway, you'll have plenty of time to revise the plan. We have to do it again in the spring anyway, when the new food shipments are set up and delivered to Cathode."

The Baron sighed and walked into the main room of the redoubt, followed by Lil Red's laughter.

The Scorched Earth
Introduction

The Scorched Earth is a collection of tales of a future gone terribly wrong. "Lil Red and The Baron" and "Drucy's Tale" are two stories of the exploration of that future, a post-apocalyptic setting in which our future civilizations were destroyed by a fire in the atmosphere, which burned over all of the known world. Humans escaped into underground or underwater vaults and into orbit. Ages passed while the fires raged, and civilizations rearranged themselves into new forms to suit the whims or fears of those who led them.

The underground denizens have once again returned to the surface and learned anew how to live on the face of the planet. Their civilizations again have adapted, and there are vast disparities between them – and even within them. They face antagonistic neighbors, creatures formed during the harshest times on the planet, and the genetic mutations introduced (either purposefully or not) since the time of the burning.

Partial Lexicon

Alloy Cross, The – 1) A small paramilitary organization promoting the return to "family values" during the pre-Scorching era (oldspeak). 2) A high-tech sect of the Children of Man, firmly ensconced in the ConFed, as its religious and moral advisers (newspeak).

Aqua – 1) Undersea habitat built by the Confederation of Five Nations (oldspeak). 2) A high-tech and isolationist undersea faction of the Children of Man, with great leaps in the areas of genetic engineering and construction (newspeak). 3) One of the Sea Kingdoms, located of the west coast of Northam (newspeak).

Barrow Wights – A term for those people, animals and communities that emerged from the Vault with mutations and genetic damage, either through exposure or genetic tampering (newspeak slang).

Brotherhood of Steel, The – The military arm of Missionary-Soldiers serving The Alloy Cross (newspeak).

Children of Man – The collected human survivors of the Scorching (newspeak).

Children of the Scorching, The – A term for the rare new species that has arisen after the Scorching. Some of the Children of the Scorching are sentient (newspeak).

Chip-Lock – A high-tech lock that uses small beams of light instead of tumblers. Key-Chips have several ports that bend or block the light at certain frequencies. If the right configuration is found, the lock opens. Chip-locks are almost impossible to defeat unless using a device such as a Raffles (oldspeak).

ConFed, The – 1) A term for the Confederation of Five Nations (oldspeak slang). 2) A high-tech faction of the Children of Man controlling the northeast and central east portions of Northam. The ConFed is a fascist state, governed by the Commander in Chief and his Cabinet and supported by the Alloy Cross and its Brotherhood of Steel (newspeak).

Confederation of Five Nations, The – Pre-Scorching union comprised of the United States of America, The United Tribes of Africa, England, The Irish/Scottish Republic and The Russian Republics (oldspeak).

Gauss Gun – 1) A linear accelerated ballistic weapon used as long-rang artillery (old speak). 2) Any Gauss weapon (newspeak slang).

Gauss Weapon – A weapon that uses a linear magnetic barrel to fire small projectiles ranging from drug-coated needles to high-explosive anti-vehicular rounds (old speak). Known for their longer range than most ballistic weapons, as well as their finicky nature and constant need of maintenance. Also known as a "rail gun."

Kay – Term for one thousand units of currency or barter goods (newspeak slang).

Lazgun – A term for any laser-based weapon (newspeak slang).

Lazweapon – A high-tech weapon firing a pulse or

beam of coherent light stimulated by various forms of radiation (i.e. laser; oldspeak). Lazweapons come in many shapes and sizes, and most can be set for either a high-energy pulse or low-energy stream. Lazweapons, regardless of the type of radiation used (gamma, x-ray, microwave, etc.) tend to be invisible and almost completely without sound, and have an extended range of effectiveness. However, conditions such as fog, rain, even aerosols designed refract the beam make lazweapons specialized combat weapons at best.

Power Gun – 1) A short-ranged, energy-based rifle that emits a focused wave of kinetic energy in a shotgun-like spread (old speak). Settings can be as low as to knock over a small object or powerful enough to punch through a concrete wall, depending of the energy expended per shot. Weapons of this type are extremely power consuming and unpredictable in effect (oldspeak). 2) Any "physical force" based weapon (newspeak slang).

Raffles – A thief's tool designed to cheat chip-locks. It uses a configurable probe that reconfigures several times a second, faster that the lock can detect an erroneous code (newspeak slang).

Scorched Earth, The – The term the Children of Man use for the planet (newspeak).

Scorching, The – An environmental disaster of unknown origin, the Scorching nearly managed to destroy all life on the face of Earth (newspeak).

Sea Kingdoms, The – A union of the cities of Nu-lantis, Aqua and other underwater cities, formed after the Scorching.

Spyder Domain, The – A high-tech faction of the Children of Man, with an elevated degree of genetic engineering skills. The Domain maintains a decadent slave culture that professes enlightenment through exploring pleasure and pain. Domains are each ruled by a "queen" and are scattered about the globe (newspeak).

Vault – 1) An underground city/bunker designed originally by the Confederation of Five Nations (but soon copied by most nations of the Earth) to allow humanity to survive the Scorching (oldspeak). 2) Any underground emplacement (newspeak slang).

About the Authors

Allen Wold

Allen Wold was born in south-western Michigan, where he began writing when he discovered an old portable typewriter in his back closet. He finished high school in Tucson, Arizona, and graduated from Pomona College, in Claremont, California, where he later met his wife, Diane. They married in 1972, and moved to North Carolina, where he began his career as a full time writer. In 1986, he became a full time father, writing when he could make the time. In 2003, he became a full time writer again, when his daughter, Darcy, went off to college, also at Pomona.

Currently, Allen is still working on his epic heroic fantasy (3000 pages, 800,000 words); a vampire novel (no twinklies) in submission; a bizarre haunted house story that is far too long; and other projects in hand.

Other publications include:

- The *Rikard Braeth* series;
- The Planet Masters
- Star God
- The Eye in the Stone
- Contributions to the "V" Series
- Five non-fiction books on computers
- several short stories (mostly for the *Elf Quest* anthologies)
- a number of articles, columns, reviews, etc., also concerning computers;
- *Cat Tales,* a short collection of essays
- *A Closet for a Dragon and Other Early Tales,* a collection of short stories
- *Stroad's Cross*, a haunted village novel

Most of Allen's books are available from or through Amazon.com.

Allen has been running his version of a writer's workshop at various conventions for more than thirty years, and has had some success, since several people have not only finished but sold stories started in the workshop. He also runs a plotting workshop, an interactive lecture, which is a lot of fun, and which people have found helpful.

Allen is a member of SFWA.

Sergey Gerasimov

Sergey Gerasimov is a resident of Ukraine where he enjoys playing tennis when not writing. He has a degree in theoretical physics from Kharkov University.

Other publications include:

- "The Glory of the World", in Clarkesworld Magazine
- "The Most Dangerous Profession", in Fantasy Magazine
- "Speaking About Pancakes", in Strange Horizons
- "A Technological Forecast", in Adbusters Magazine, #71,
- "Sweaty, Fat Nightmare", in Adbusters Magazine, #68
- "Sunset in the Gulf of Cyclopses", in Oceans of the Mind,
- "Terra Fantastica", Optimism in literature around the world, and SF in particular, part 1
- "The Load of Study", in AlienSkin Magazine
- "The Glory of the World", Realms 2: The Second Year of Clarkesworld Magazine
- "The Glory of the World", in "The Apex Book of World SF"
- Approximately a hundred stories, in books and magazines, in Russia and Ukraine.

Michelle Herndon

Michelle Herndon is a resident of Black Mountain, North Carolina, and enjoys writing, sushi, anime, and world domination.

She has a BFA in English from Western Carolina University; a PhD in religion and zoology from Miskatonic University; and she is working on a graduate degree in physics from the Xavier Institute for Higher Learning. In her spare time she works in a bookstore when not hunting vampires.

Other publications include:

- "Winter's Hold" originally published in the Phase 5 Monthly Review
- "What a Shame" originally published in the Phase 5 Monthly Review

K.R. Gentile

K.R. Gentile is an unwilling resident of Asheville, North Carolina and enjoys zeppelins, clockwork minions, warbot A.I.s, and secret volcano bases.

Other publications include:

- "The Tale-Seller's Night", a tale of The Scorched Earth, originally published in the *Phase 5 Monthly Review*
- *...The Colour of Time*, a supervillain novella published by Phase 5

James McCarthy

James McCarthy is originally from Kalamazoo, Michigan in the 1950s, and was part of the first generation of kids raised on television. Besides cartoons and comedies, he enjoyed the fantasy and science fiction shows. He also has fond memories of having multiple seasons, and has a special love for the snow and ice of winter, which he sees little of in his current home in Brandon, Florida.

He cites those childhood memories to be a great source of inspiration now, especially when listening to music: prog rock, classical, fusion jazz, new age, electronic and medieval. He has been seriously painting since 1999, and has exhibited artwork in galleries in the Tampa Bay area.

He graduated from Tampa Catholic High School and majored in painting at the University of South Florida. After school, he worked at Design/Art, a commercial art studio in Tampa which was run by his father, for 25 years until it closed in 2001.

James is also the artist of thirteen art pieces listed below, which will accompany his short story, "The Observatory Gardens" in a story book forthcoming from Phase 5.

Other publications include several illustrations published by Foster Friends, a local children's book company.

Arnold Cassell

Arnold Cassell is a resident of Minnesota and enjoys games and stories.

You can check out his podcasts on YouTube.

Nanna P. Vej

Nanna P. Vej is stuck in Denmark, where she is a student, though she hopes to escape as soon as possible.

She enjoys writing, reading and watching various TV-shows and movies.

Learn more about and stay updated with our Authors at www.phase5publishing.com

Other Books from Phase 5

Sheleasoun:
Book I of Beneath the Echoes of Memory

A light fantasy adventure novel by Brandy Wayne
Cover art, *Darra*, by Tesa Gunawan

Darra dreams of breaking out of her stifling life, but when
her home is attacked, her parents taken, and she
discovers she's inherited a "gift" which could get her killed,
she embarks on a mission that will change her life forever
- and her place in the world around her.
Accompanied by woodsmen as odd as she is, she
discovers that friends can be your enemies, power can be
circumvented, and the villains in the stories her father told
her as a child are nothing compared to the monsters that
roam the land on two legs.
And there are miracles.

Classification: Fantasy/Teen Fantasy
Appropriate for Teens and Adults: Non-graphic Violence &
Death, Infrequent Mild Cursing

Phase 5 Elements: Sn 81 Supernatural; Sv 301 Super-
villain; Dc 5 Death Cult

ISBN: 978-0-9835795-4-0 Trade Paperback,
5.5"x8.5", 280 pages
ISBN: 978-0-9835795-5-7 e-book

Nerve Zero

A zero-g noir novel by Justin Robinson
Cover art, *Hinden & Typhon*, by Ralph J. Ryan

Idriel Ramirez has returned home, haunted by the shame
of being a conscripted pilot for the New Terran Empire.
Haunted by the shame that he's felt the sky.
Once respected as a nerve, now he's just pressed.
Few in Hinden, clouded jewel of a fallen empire,
will even look him in the eye.
Drawn into crime and mystery by Ausiel Montoya,
an old itch, Ramirez tells himself he's floating
through Hinden's steel nest of assassins,
psychos and cultists because of what the money
she promised can buy him - years off his indenture.
But as he delves deeper into the heart of his wretched
homeworld
he finds the secret she's carrying is as big as the secret at
core of Hinden.
And just as dangerous.

Classification: Science Fiction
Appropriate for adults: Variant violence, Death, Infrequent
cursing, Non-graphic deviant sexual situations

Phase 5 Elements: Human Derivative 13, Another World
101, Noir 0

ISBN: 978-0-9835795-2-6 $10.95 Trade Paperback
5.5"x8.5", 279 pages
ISBN: 978-0-9835795-3-3 $4.95 ebook

...The Colour of Time

A super-villain novelette by K.R. Gentile
Cover art, *Divine Blessing* by Dylan Hansen

Psychopharmacologist.

Super-spy.

Master assassin.

Cult leader.

...Devoted Godson?

This is the unauthorized biography
of the infamous super-villain,
Dr. Peppermint.

Classification: Science Fiction/Fantasy
Appropriate for Adults Only: Violence, death, brief, mildly-
graphic sexual situations, frequent cursing.

Phase 5 Elements: Sn 81 Supernatural; Sv 301 Super-
villain; Dc 5 Death Cult

ISBN: 978-0-9835795-4-0 Trade Paperback,
5.5"x8.5", 38 pages
ISBN: 978-0-9835795-5-7 e-book

The Solution

A horror novella by Rick McQuiston
Cover art, *Undead Horizon*, by Dylan Hansen

Brad survived the raid on his home weeks ago,
but now is trapped with a strange little girl.

Dr. Vinheiser has not been himself for too long,
and now his time is running out.

An unnatural evil taunts and twists everything
to fuel its work, to fulfill its purpose.

A cruel and voracious leader seeks a prize
of great power, but remains cautious.

Something here is wrong.

Classification: Horror
Appropriate for Teens and Adults: Non-graphic violence
and death; evil object; addiction; unromantic vampires

Phase 5 Elements: In 104 - Invasion; Fk 111 - Forbidden
knowledge; Dr 89 - Dimensional rift

ISBN: 978-0-9835795-7-1 Paperback,
4.37"x7", 108 pages
ISBN: 978-0-9835795-6-4 e-book

CPSIA information can be obtained
at www.ICGtesting.com
Printed in the USA
BVHW052143240423
662988BV00013B/295